Dear Reader,

I can't believe my lease is up at Bachelor Arms this month! Writing in this series has been a real treat for me. This month, you'll meet bachelor number three, the sexy Garrett McCabe, in *A Happily Unmarried Man*.

I had to give this consummate bachelor a great heroine— the ultimate homemaker, Emily Taylor. In this respect, Emily bears absolutely no resemblance to me. When I'm writing, housework seems to take a back seat to deadlines. But Emily does share my passion for "projects." I've planted a perennial garden and I do a bit of gourmet cooking on occasion. And I've personally painted or papered every single wall in my eighty-year-old house. Some of them twice! Now, if I could just find the time to drywall that upstairs bathroom....

I hope you enjoy reading *A Happily Unmarried Man* as much as I enjoyed writing it. I'd love to hear your comments about all my Bachelor Arms heroes and heroines—Tru and Caroline, Josh and Taryn, and Garrett and Emily. You can write to me in care of Harlequin Books.

Sincerely,

Kate Hoffmann

c/o Harlequin Temptation
225 Duncan Mill Road
Don Mills, Ontario M3B 3K9
Canada

BACHELOR ARMS

Come live and love in L.A. with the tenants of Bachelor Arms

Bachelor Arms is a trendy apartment building with some very colorful tenants. Meet three confirmed bachelors who are determined to stay single until three very special women turn their lives upside down; college friends who reunite to plan a wedding; a cynical and sexy lawyer; a director who's renowned for his hedonistic life-style, and many more...including one very mysterious and legendary tenant. And while everyone tries to ignore the legend, every once in a while something strange happens....

Each of these fascinating people has a tale of success or failure, love or heartbreak. But their stories don't stay a secret for long in the hallways of Bachelor Arms.

Bachelor Arms is a captivating place, home to an eclectic group of neighbors. All of them have one thing in common, though—the feeling of community that is very much a part of living at Bachelor Arms.

BACHELOR ARMS

BACHELOR HUSBAND   February 1995
Kate Hoffmann

THE STRONG SILENT TYPE   March 1995
Kate Hoffmann

A HAPPILY UNMARRIED MAN   April 1995
Kate Hoffmann

NEVER A BRIDE   May 1995
JoAnn Ross

FOR RICHER OR POORER   June 1995
JoAnn Ross

THREE GROOMS AND A WEDDING July 1995
JoAnn Ross

LOVERS AND STRANGERS   August 1995
Candace Schuler

SEDUCED AND BETRAYED   September 1995
Candace Schuler

PASSION AND SCANDAL   October 1995
Candace Schuler

THE LADY IN THE MIRROR   November 1995
Judith Arnold

TIMELESS LOVE   December 1995
Judith Arnold

THE TENANTS OF BACHELOR ARMS

Ken Amberson: The odd superintendent who knows more than he admits about the legend of Bachelor Arms.

Josh Banks: The strong, silent type. A financial whiz who is more comfortable with numbers than with women.

Eddie Cassidy: Local bartender at Flynn's next door. He's looking for his big break as a screenwriter.

Jill Foyle: This sexy, recently divorced interior designer moved to L.A. to begin a new life.

Tru Hallihan: A loner P.I. who loves 'em and leaves 'em.

Natasha Kuryan: This elderly Russian-born femme fatale was a makeup artist to the stars of yesterday.

Garrett McCabe: A confirmed bachelor whose newspaper column touts the advantages of single life.

Brenda Muir: Young, enthusiastic would-be actress who supports herself as a waitress.

Bobbie-Sue O'Hara: Brenda's best friend. She works as an actress and waitress but knows that real power lies on the other side of the camera.

Bob Robinson: This barfly seems to live at Flynn's and has an opinion about everyone and everything.

Theodore "Teddy" Smith: The resident Lothario—any new female in the building puts a sparkle in his eye.

A HAPPILY UNMARRIED MAN

KATE HOFFMANN

Harlequin Books

TORONTO • NEW YORK • LONDON
AMSTERDAM • PARIS • SYDNEY • HAMBURG
STOCKHOLM • ATHENS • TOKYO • MILAN
MADRID • WARSAW • BUDAPEST • AUCKLAND

If you purchased this book without a cover you should be aware that this book is stolen property. It was reported as "unsold and destroyed" to the publisher, and neither the author nor the publisher has received any payment for this "stripped book."

To Pesha Rubinstein, my favorite agent, whose enthusiasm for my stories made writing them all the more fun

ISBN 0-373-25633-7

A HAPPILY UNMARRIED MAN

Copyright © 1995 by Peggy Hoffmann.

All rights reserved. Except for use in any review, the reproduction or utilization of this work in whole or in part in any form by any electronic, mechanical or other means, now known or hereafter invented, including xerography, photocopying and recording, or in any information storage or retrieval system, is forbidden without the written permission of the publisher, Harlequin Enterprises Limited, 225 Duncan Mill Road, Don Mills, Ontario, Canada M3B 3K9.

All characters in this book have no existence outside the imagination of the author and have no relation whatsoever to anyone bearing the same name or names. They are not even distantly inspired by any individual known or unknown to the author, and all incidents are pure invention.

This edition published by arrangement with Harlequin Enterprises B.V.

® and TM are trademarks of the publisher. Trademarks indicated with ® are registered in the United States Patent and Trademark Office, the Canadian Trade Marks Office and in other countries.

Printed in U.S.A.

1

"WHAT COLOR UNDERWEAR does she wear?" Garrett Mc-
Cabe dragged his gaze from the window display of the lingerie store to study the unnerved expression of his com-
panion, Josh Banks.

Leave it to Josh to be disconcerted by the mere mention
of ladies' unmentionables. The third window shopper in the
group, Tru Hallihan, leaned over and sent Garrett a re-
proachful glare from the other side of Josh, then turned back
to his careful perusal of a sheer purple nightie.

Josh looked over his shoulder at the Saturday morning
crowd of shoppers at the Beverly Center, as if worried
someone might overhear Garrett's rather indelicate query.
"I believe that's something that should remain between me
and my wife," he replied evenly.

"Suit yourself. But I've made a very careful study of
women's underwear," Garrett continued, "and I've developed some rather interesting theories."

"This should be good," Tru muttered.

"In fact, if you remember, I explored this very important
issue in my column. I believe underwear color is an important indicator of a woman's personality type. There's your
red underwear type, daring, but too controlling for my
tastes. Women who wear white underwear are often sexu-
ally repressed and overly practical. Flowered underwear?
Keep your distance, airhead ahead. And then there are those
who wear black. They—"

"Taryn wears black," Josh offered.

Garrett smiled. "Lucky man. Uninhibited and adventurous. So go inside and get Taryn something in black. Something like that little item right there." He pointed to a lacy black bustier.

Josh blinked behind his conservative, wire-rimmed glasses, then straightened his Brooks Brothers tie. "You want me to go inside and buy that—that—I'm not sure I know what that thing is called."

"Bustier. And I thought you needed an anniversary present," Garrett said.

Josh turned back to the window and examined the item in question. "It looks a little, ah, uncomfortable. Have you guys ever really been with a woman who has worn something like this?"

Tru shoved his hands into the pockets of his battered leather jacket. "Never," he sighed.

"Me neither," Josh said, perplexed.

They both watched Garrett with baited breath. He considered his response carefully. After all, he did have a reputation to protect. He was Garrett McCabe, author of the popular "Boys' Night Out," a twice weekly newspaper column extolling the virtues of manhood—mostly of the bachelor persuasion. He was considered L.A.'s most confirmed bachelor. But image was a little further from reality than he'd care to publicly admit.

Of the three, he was now the only unmarried one left in the group. Tru, a former private investigator, had wed radio marriage counselor Caroline Leighton nearly three months before. And Josh, a tax accountant, had taken the plunge just a few weeks ago in Las Vegas, marrying artist and jet-setting party girl, Taryn Wilde.

Until recently, Tru, Josh, and Garrett had each resided alone at the Bachelor Arms, an apartment building with a rather colorful past. Now, Tru lived with Caroline in her

Laurel Canyon home and Taryn lived with Josh in his Arms apartment. Only the occasional lunch and their regular Tuesday night poker game at Flynn's kept them in touch.

Garrett couldn't help but regret his friends' marriages. Though both Caroline and Taryn were lovely women, he had always thought he and Josh and Tru would remain bachelors forever. But obviously he was the only one who truly cherished his single status. For Garrett, bachelorhood meant absolute freedom. And relationships with women came purely on his own terms.

Garrett turned his gaze away from the bustier. "To be honest, I have never had the pleasure of meeting a woman of such . . . discriminating taste," Garrett replied. "But that doesn't mean I haven't stopped looking."

It wasn't that Garrett had any bad examples of marriage to draw upon. In fact, he came from a long line of happily married people. His parents, his grandparents, each one of his seven brothers and sisters, all of them had strong, vital marriages. Blissful wedlock had turned into a damn family tradition and they brought more than a little pressure to bear on Garrett to continue the tradition.

From the time he was a child, it was assumed that he would marry and have a family, settle down in a nice home in the suburbs of Boston with a few kids and a dog. That he didn't care to, even at the ripe old age of thirty-five, was a source of unending speculation.

Holidays at home in Boston had turned into hellish inquisitions with any number of blind dates arranged. He no longer tried to explain his choice and in some ways he believed he remained steadfastly single just to spite his interfering family. All he really knew was that the marriage bug would not bite this McCabe.

"I think you should buy it, Josh. You won't regret it," Garrett said.

Josh frowned. "I had something more . . . traditional in mind. Aren't there certain gifts one gives on anniversaries? You know, twenty-five is silver and fifty is gold. What do I give for two weeks?"

"I think two weeks is traditionally peekaboo underwear," Garrett explained. "A month is edible panties. Then, at two months, the thoughtful husband gives black leather."

Josh glanced over to Tru for confirmation and Hallihan shook his head. "Maybe we should try another store," Josh concluded. "I have a feeling this anniversary stuff is important and I don't want to mess up this early in my marriage."

"All right," Garrett said. "But let's make it quick. I've got a column to write before five and I still don't have a clue as to my subject. Why don't we try the bookstore up on eight? A cookbook might be nice."

Josh's expression brightened. "A cookbook? Taryn's trying to learn how to cook. I—I think that would be best." He took one final longing look at the lingerie then headed for the escalator.

The Beverly Center was the crown jewel in all of Los Angeles malldom—three levels of shops built from muted taupe-colored marble and high-tech glass, enhanced by piped-in music and exotic fast-food odors wafting through the climate-controlled air. Every non-essential item known to man was for sale in one store or another.

Garrett hated shopping malls, even more than he hated the dentist's office. Whatever it was that women found so fascinating about 170 stores stacked eight stories above the street had completely eluded him. Maybe it was in the genes. Where men were blessed with an X and Y chromosome, women had an X and M, the M being the little bugger that made shopping malls tolerable. He'd even written a column on it once.

As the escalator approached the eighth floor, Garrett noticed a long line of shoppers winding through the mall. He traced the line back to its source—the bookstore. "I think you might want to consider perfume, Josh. The bookstore looks a little busy." Garrett squinted to read the banner above the store's entrance. "Some author named Emily Taylor. She's autographing her newest book."

Tru's gaze snapped around to the banner. "Emily Taylor? Caroline's got all her books. She's always reading them in bed."

"How flattering," Garrett teased. "For you, I mean."

"Is she that *At Home* lady?" Josh asked.

"Yeah, that's her magazine," Tru said. "*Emily Taylor At Home*."

"I think Taryn reads that magazine," Josh said. "She's got a pile of them from her grandmother stacked on the kitchen counter and she won't let me throw them away."

"Who is Emily Taylor?" Garrett asked.

"I guess she's a housewife," Tru replied. "A professional housewife."

"I didn't know there was such a thing," Garrett said. "So, could I hire her to take care of my apartment? And all my other needs? You know, laundry, shopping . . ."

Josh shook his head. "According to Taryn, Emily Taylor has turned homemaking into an art. Taryn's been trying to emulate Emily in the kitchen, though I think she'd be better off sticking to what she does best—microwave popcorn and orange juice."

"You've got it easy. Caroline is into gardening which means *I'm* into gardening," Tru explained. "We've spent the last four weekends shopping for perennials. I've hauled at least a ton of topsoil from the car to the yard and I missed the Lakers game last Saturday while I helped her try to figure out what the soil pH was. She says we're going to have an English border garden just like Emily's."

"Taryn tried to make a shower curtain for the bathroom out of a lace tablecloth," Josh went on. "When I told her we had plenty of money to buy a real shower curtain, she told me that wasn't the point. Then she started crying and told me I didn't appreciate her efforts and she was a failure as a wife. And then she made me eat a casserole with artichokes in it." Josh shuddered. "I hate it when she cries. And I hate artichokes."

Garrett scowled. "I can't believe what I'm hearing. It sounds like you're both letting this Emily Taylor run your life."

"It's not that bad," Josh said. "At least, not yet. Taryn just thinks she needs a little help being a proper wife. I'll bet she'd like an autographed book for an anniversary present."

"We'd better get in line," Tru replied. "If Caroline finds out I was this close to Emily Taylor and didn't bring her a book, she'll have me shoveling sheep manure for the next month."

Tru and Josh headed for the end of the line, a line composed exclusively of chattering women. Garrett stared at them in disbelief, then followed. If they were joking with him, he didn't find this particularly amusing. And if they weren't, he was seriously worried about the mental health of his two best friends.

"Come on guys," he muttered. "I can't believe you two are going to wait in line for an autographed book by a professional housewife. She's a housewife, boys, not an all-star pitcher, not an MVP point guard." Garrett shook his head in disgust. "This is not funny."

"Just wait," Tru said.

"For what?" Garrett asked. "This?"

"For the smile on your wife's face when you do something special for her," Tru said. "There's nothing like it, McCabe. It's like looking at a little piece of heaven."

"I like being married," Josh said. "Taryn makes life . . . exciting."

"I'm planning to remain happily unmarried for the rest of my life, thank you," Garrett stated.

Tru and Josh glanced at each other and smiled conspiratorially.

"What?" Garrett demanded. "You don't think it's possible?"

"Sure, I guess it is. But what about the woman in the mirror?" Tru asked.

Garrett shifted uneasily and crossed his arms. "What woman?"

"The ghost," Josh prodded. "The one you saw in the mirror in Tru's old apartment. In 1-G. Don't you remember what Eddie and Bob told us about the legend?"

Garrett remembered exactly what the ridiculous legend was all about—and what an imaginative bartender and his favorite barfly had said. The mirror and the ghost appeared only to those who would soon have their deepest fear or their greatest dream come to pass. No one seemed to know which.

Strange stories of ghosts, of murder and intrigue and suicide, had swirled around the history of the Bachelor Arms for years, perpetuated by rumor and exaggeration, until even *he* had imagined a vision in the mirror. But there was no ghost, only an old mirror and some silly story that went along with it, and two friends with a warped sense of humor.

"Don't tell me you two really believe in all that stuff," Garrett said.

"Sure," Tru admitted. "I saw the ghost. So did Josh."

Garrett held up his hands in mock surrender. "All right, I'll play your little game. I'll admit it. I've hallucinated a woman or two in my bedroom after a few too many beers at Flynn's. But a lady ghost in a mirror? No way."

"You may scoff now," Tru teased. "But you'll find out later."

"Maybe so. But right now, all I really want to find out is why a professional housewife named Emily Taylor is determined to domesticate every man on this planet. In fact, I think I smell a column here."

"I wouldn't take on Emily Taylor," Josh whispered, glancing around at the women that surrounded them. "You'd might as well take on the entire female race."

"I'm not scared of some frumpy little housewife," Garrett murmured. "What's she going to do, put arsenic in a batch of oatmeal cookies and force me to eat them? Or maybe she'll beat me over the head with a sponge mop."

By this time, they'd reached the entrance to the store and the line in front of them was considerably shorter. Garrett craned his neck to catch a glimpse of the ultimate homemaker. A plump, dark-haired woman sat at a table fifteen feet in front of him. Her hair was twisted into a haphazard knot on the top of her head and she wore an unflattering pair of wire-rimmed glasses that perched on the end of her nose. She looked as if she belonged on a cake box. Exactly what he expected.

Garrett grabbed a copy of *Emily Taylor's Summer at the Shore* from a nearby table and flipped through it. Just what he needed—a guide for alfresco entertaining and barbecue. The last time he remembered eating alfresco was wolfing down a hot dog and guzzling a beer in between innings of a Dodgers game. He flipped through the pages and smiled. Perfect little picnics on perfect little plates and not an ant in sight. Who *was* this woman anyway? The self-annointed high priestess of parties?

A perfect little pigeon, Garrett mused. Plump, plucked and ready to be barbecued—alfresco—in the next installment of "Boys' Night Out." In an instant the words seemed to flood his mind and he was tempted to find a piece of paper and get it all down.

But first, he'd get a good look at this paragon of pigeonhood. As Josh and Tru stepped aside, their autographed copies clutched in their arms, Garrett moved up to the table. He held the book out to the dark-haired Ms. Taylor. She looked at him with a weary expression then cocked her head to the left.

"Just sign it 'To the best writer I've ever known,'" Garrett requested.

She shook her head nervously, then rolled her eyes not once but twice.

Garrett frowned. What was wrong with her? She seemed awfully twitchy for a paragon. Maybe she'd been sniffing too much furniture polish. He cursed inwardly. From a professional standpoint, it wasn't considered cool to make fun of someone so outwardly odd, someone with such a pronounced... facial tick. Her head snapped to the left again.

"What was that you wanted Ms. Taylor to inscribe?" she asked sweetly. She snatched the book from his hand and slid it over to the woman sitting next to her, a woman he hadn't even noticed.

Garrett's gaze shifted over to the quiet figure on the left. No wonder he hadn't noticed her. On first glance, she appeared painfully plain, like a faded wallflower. But then, as he met her startling green eyes, he felt compelled to take a closer look.

Surrounded by a halo of curly red hair that just brushed her shoulders, her pale, delicate features seemed almost frozen in place. She wore an unflattering flowered dress with a white lace-edged collar that did nothing to reveal the figure beneath. She didn't smile, just watched him with a remoteness in her eyes, almost like a mannequin in a shop window.

"*You're* Emily Taylor?" Garrett asked.

"Yes, this is Emily Taylor," the dark-haired woman confirmed. "She's very glad to meet you. Now what would you like her to inscribe in your book?"

"I thought you—I mean, she's—" He glanced down at Emily again, but she now stared at her neatly folded hands, aloof and uninterested in any explanation for his mistake.

"Emily Taylor," her assistant said. "I believe we've covered that already."

He held out his hand and Emily's gaze jumped up to his. "You're not what I expected," he explained. She still didn't return his smile, nor did she offer her hand in return. Garrett felt a distinct chill in the air.

"I'm afraid Ms. Taylor doesn't have the time for conversation right now," her assistant explained. "There are many people waiting to see her. Please, move along."

"But she hasn't signed my book yet," Garrett said, his gaze still pinned to hers.

Emily blinked, then opened the book and signed it in a precise script. She presented it to Garrett right along with an artificial smile.

"Thank you," she murmured tersely before she dropped her gaze back to her hands.

Garrett smiled. "No," he replied. "Thank *you*."

Tru and Josh waited at the magazine rack, Tru perusing a copy of *Real-Life Detective* and Josh reading an article in *Business Week*. As he approached, Garrett rubbed his arms dramatically and shivered. "Is it a little cold in here, or is it just me?"

Josh glanced around, his brow furrowed. "I don't feel cold. Actually, I'm quite comfortable."

Tru chuckled and shoved the magazine back on the rack. "What's wrong, McCabe?" he asked. "Didn't she melt under your considerable charm?"

Josh's confusion deepened as he fumbled to replace his reading material. "Melt?"

"Emily Taylor," Garrett explained as he grinned and slapped her book against his thigh. "What a piece of work that lady is. Gentlemen, I believe I'm no longer in search of a subject. I'm going to roast that frosty little domestic goddess in the next edition of 'Boys' Night Out.' Come on, let's get out of here. I've got a column to write."

"I'M NOT GOING BACK out there," Emily said, her voice desperate. She backed up against a tall metal rack stacked with books and wove her fingers through the wire mesh shelves.

If she could have, she would have chained herself to the rack or locked herself in the dismal little bathroom. "All those people. There were even men out there! And they kept talking to me. I didn't know what to say." The storeroom was silent for a long moment and Emily began to think that she'd finally persuaded her best friend and business partner, Nora Griswold, to forget her grandiose promotional ideas.

"Em, they're your fans. They love you. They just want a chance to meet you. Besides, you know how well your books sell in California. Who did you think was buying them?"

Emily pulled a book off the shelf and covered her face with it. "I'm a fraud," she said. "I feel like some snake oil salesman. And if I have to face them, they're going to figure it out. They think Emily is the epitome of contemporary homemaking, not some bag of neuroses."

Nora grabbed the book and tossed it onto a small card table. "You're not a fraud," she countered. "You're brilliant at what you do and women all over this country love and respect you. You've turned homemaking into a desirable profession. Just look at all the working women who read your books and magazines and wish they had the time to stay home and work on your projects."

"Then what are they doing here? Why aren't they at home where they should be, hand painting gift-wrap paper and mastering meringue? I'm just a regular person, Nora, with a minor talent for arts and crafts...and cooking...and gardening and decorating. They act like I'm someone important."

"You are. You're an important person with a severe self-confidence problem."

"You go out there," Emily ordered. "You sign those books and talk to all those strangers. You try to sound intelligent when your heart is stuck in your throat and you feel like bursting into tears."

"They don't want to see me, they want to see Emily Taylor."

"Why is this happening?" Emily cried, running her fingers through her unruly copper hair. "I never wanted things to get so...so big! I just wanted to write a few simple *anonymous* how-to books. I wasn't even interested in the magazine until you talked me into it. Nora, I'm just a housewife from Rhode Island. I have no education, no job experience. I don't even have a husband anymore. I can't be the celebrity you want me to be."

"Like it or not, you are a celebrity, Em. And you need to start acting like one. It's important to show Parker Publishing that you're behind the magazine. That you're willing to promote your name."

Emily flopped down onto a folding chair and began to methodically stuff her mouth from the plate of shortbread cookies the bookstore manager had left for them. They weren't homemade, but they *were* English. She could tell. She'd done an article on shortbread in the November issue and had personally tasted every variety available in the States, then taught her readers how to make their own from a recipe she'd developed. She'd even spent a week in England, haunting every antique shop within a hundred-mile radius of London in search of shortbread molds. "Tell me again why we have to sell *At Home*," she said as she munched on a cookie. "I like working with Arnie Wilson. He's never made me do book signings or personal appearances."

"Arnie has been a wonderful publisher and partner," Nora explained. "But he's ready to retire and Richard Parker has the financial resources to make *At Home* a power in the marketplace. We should be thrilled he's even bothered to look at our little magazine. We won't have to operate on a shoestring any more, Em. And we'll never have to worry about whether there will be enough left over for our paychecks."

"It hasn't been that bad, has it, Nora? We've always been able to make it work."

"But Parker can make it work better. Em, he's going to make you a household name."

"I *am* a household name already and I hate it. I just want to work on my projects in peace and quiet."

"This is all Eric's fault you know," Nora said.

"What does my ex-husband have to do with this?"

"Your ex-slimeball has *everything* to do with this. He's the one who's destroyed your self-confidence."

Emily sighed and grabbed another cookie. "Don't start with your amateur psychoanalysis again, Nora. I've heard this all before. Every time you start seeing a new shrink or taking a new class, you find a new explanation for all my so-called problems. I'm just a little shy."

"Compared to you, Howard Hughes was a party animal," Nora quipped, grabbing what was left of the cookies. "You should try analysis or at least take an assertiveness training course. Even a yoga class would be good. I personally believe self-improvement is the key to happiness."

Emily daintily wiped the crumbs from her mouth with a paper napkin, then refolded it neatly. "I'm just a little shy," she repeated. "I don't need a shrink to tell me that. I've always been shy, ever since I was a little girl."

"You didn't say more than twenty words out there. Half of them were *thank* and the other half were *you*. People expect Emily Taylor to be bright and bubbly. This is the woman who taught us all how to make peach potpourri and authentic Louisiana pralines. You taught us how to stencil our floors and stipple our walls. You showed us how to turn simple entertaining into a memorable event. Em, you are going to have to get a hold of yourself and learn to deal with your public."

"All right!" Emily said, attempting to sound determined. She pushed to her feet, then suddenly felt dizzy with panic. The shortbread felt like a lump of lead in her stomach. "I feel much better now," she croaked. "Let's go out there and sign some more books."

"Actually, there's one more thing we need to discuss. Now that you're all gung ho to face the masses."

Emily sat back down. "What is it, Nora? You didn't arrange another one of these horrid book signings, did you? I just can't do this again. Please, please, don't make me."

"No, it's a party. Richard Parker has arranged a small gathering in honor of your visit to Los Angeles and the upcoming negotiations for the sale of *At Home.*"

"How small?" Emily asked.

"Small," Nora assured her.

"Be precise, please. Knowing you, Mardi Gras might be considered an intimate little get-together."

"I didn't ask him for a head count."

Emily fixed Nora with a watered-down glare. They'd been best friends for so long that Nora was the only person in the world Emily could pretend to stand up to without dissolving into a fit of insecurity and guilt.

"Around a hundred," Nora admitted. "But, it's at his home in Beverly Hills."

"At his home? Oh, that makes me feel so much better. I hope he has a good lock on the bathroom door, because that's exactly where I plan to spend most of the evening." Emily braced her elbows on the table in front of her and buried her face in her hands. "You *know* how I hate parties. I'm no good at chitchat. People start talking about politics and current affairs and all I want to do is sneak into the kitchen and go through the cupboards. Or rearrange the closets. Or wallpaper the pantry."

Nora patted her shoulder and Emily looked up morosely. "They're offering an assertiveness class at the Institute for Self-Improvement," Nora said. "It's called 'Just Say More!' When we get back home, you really should take it."

"Why don't you take it for me? I'm sure I'll hear about the whole thing anyway."

Nora wagged a warning finger at her. "You have a very smart mouth for someone who claims to be shy."

Mortified, Emily felt her cheeks flame. "I'm sorry," she cried. "I didn't mean to sound snippish...or ungrateful. Forgive me?"

Nora sighed and shook her head. "I was teasing, Em. Buy a sense of humor, would you? And you really should talk back a little more. It rather becomes you, my dear. You know, that red hair and those flashing green eyes." The last was said with a humorous bit of pretension. "Now, I'm going to get us both a cup of coffee at that espresso bar out in the mall and then we'll go back out there for round two. And this time, I want you to converse with your public."

"We should really do a feature on coffee," Emily said distractedly. "Coffee is *really* big right now. Cappucino, latte, mocha, and all those wonderful varieties of beans. We all take it for granted but it's such a vital part of our lives. We could include a little history of coffee and teach our readers how to make all these exotic drinks right at home. What do think?"

"I think *you* think too much about work."

"What else is there?" Emily asked.

"How about men?"

"That's your obsession, not mine." Emily felt her blush deepen. "I can't even talk to your male house cats without getting tongue-tied and flustered. What man in his right mind would possibly find me interesting?"

"How about that gorgeous hunk of manhood in the autograph line? The one who tried to shake your hand."

"Hunk? Nora, cheese comes in hunks. Men don't."

"Don't play dumb with me, Em. You know exactly who I'm talking about. That guy who tried to talk to you. The tall guy with the sun-streaked hair and the perfect nose. And that voice. Can't you just hear that voice whispering sweet nothings into your ear? He was definitely trying to pick you up. Believe me, I know these things."

"I didn't notice," Emily answered. "I was too busy hyperventilating."

Nora braced her hands on her hips and put on her long-suffering-best-friend face. "You're hopeless. Completely and utterly hopeless."

"Go get the coffee, Nora. While you're gone I'll screw up the rest of my courage and get ready to face my fans."

"Make it quick. Our fifteen-minute break is almost over."

Emily watched as Nora slipped out of the storeroom and headed back through the store. As the door swung closed, she let out a long, tightly held breath, then twisted her cramped fingers together. Nora was right. Sooner or later she'd have to learn to conquer her fears and insecurities and meet her career head-on.

But she'd never been good at head-on confrontation, even in the abstract. From the time she was a child, she'd always tried to please, hoping that her quiet manner and clever ways would gain her notice. Her father had been too busy for his only daughter and her mother had her circle of rich society friends and her charity work to occupy her time. Her three older brothers were nearly grown by the time she was born. The first person that had ever really paid attention to her was Eric.

She had married him the day after her eighteenth birthday in a huge society wedding, an event joining two old and very wealthy Newport families. They began to build a life together—a life in which Eric climbed the corporate ladder at his father's company while Emily kept the home fires burning. Eric refused to allow her to work and any talk of college was met with a laugh and an idle brush-off. With nowhere else to direct her energies, she became the best homemaker she could, taking cooking and decorating classes, turning their house into something worthy of a feature in *House Beautiful*.

She rubbed her tired eyes as if to rub away the painful memories—memories of the day her husband didn't come home. He'd left everything behind, right down to his razor and his favorite slippers. And after five years of what she thought was a happy marriage, she was left to sort through his things, as if he'd died. For a time, she allowed herself to grieve as a widow might, but then the savings gradually disappeared and the checking account went dry. She was too proud to ask Eric for a dime, and she couldn't go back to her family. They thought she was a failure. So she took the only thing she was good at and turned it into a career.

She'd always been disappointed by the how-to books available for entertaining and decorating, so she decided to write one that she'd buy herself. The first book was written at her kitchen table, and she did the sample sketches, diagrams and photos herself. *Decorating for the Holidays* passed by twelve different publishers in the course of nearly two years before she found one that would take a chance on her.

And when the tiny advance check arrived, she paid the mortgage and celebrated with a gourmet dinner for one. A month later, to her surprise, she had another contract offer, this time for two books. So she kept writing. For three years and four more books, she worked alone, and then the feminine equivalent of a middle linebacker, Nora Griswold, showed up at her front door, armed with a business proposition.

Why not turn the Emily Taylor books into a monthly magazine? Nora would set up the deal and run the magazine if Emily would put up her creativity as collateral. If it hadn't been for the balloon payment on the mortgage, Emily would have instantly refused. But Nora could be very persuasive, and even more stubborn, especially when faced with the same situation as Emily—a disappearing husband and steadily mounting debts, plus a rundown Connecticut farmhouse filled with seven hungry cats.

They found Arnie Wilson by chance after they saw a newspaper article about the monthly aviation magazine he printed and published. Nora proceeded to bully him into an agreement to print and publish *At Home* for one year. In return, Arnie was cut in for a share. Their one-year agreement quickly extended to two, then three and together they founded a little magazine that would change the face of homemaking.

Emily pushed away from the card table and stood, then smoothed her skirt with clammy palms. To soothe her nerves, she began to circle the storeroom, breathing deeply and stopping every now and then to pick up a book and flip through it.

As she made her fifth circuit around the room, she grabbed a book from the shelf labeled Self-help and began to page through Dr. Rita Carlisle's *Affirmations Made Easy*. She'd never really believed in all the pop psychobabble that Nora seemed so fond of. But after skimming just a few pages, she had to admit that there might be something more to Dr. Rita than just competition on the nonfiction bestseller lists.

"I am a confident person and I enjoy my success," Emily murmured. "I think," she added as an afterthought. "Maybe. Sometimes." With a frustrated groan and flood of embarrassment, she slapped the book shut and placed it back on the shelf. "I can't believe I'm talking to myself. Maybe I do need a shrink."

She'd circled the room three more times before she could bring herself to say the words again. "I am a confident person and I enjoy my success." This time it was easier. "I *am* a confident person and I enjoy my success. And maybe if I say it enough, I'll start to believe it. I *am* a—"

The storeroom door opened and Nora poked her head inside. "I've got the coffee. Are you ready?"

Emily nodded, gathering her resolve and trying to fight back the apprehension she always felt before facing a crowd of more than one or two.

"Who were you talking to?"

"No one important," Emily replied with a shrug, walking toward the door. *I will try to be more confident . . . and I won't throw up every time I have to be around large crowds of people.*

GARRETT GLANCED at his watch as he pushed open the front door of the Bachelor Arms. The morning sun reflected off the faded pink stucco facade and he searched his jacket pockets for his sunglasses. As he turned onto the sidewalk and headed for his parking space, he looked up at the building. Once a mansion owned by a wealthy family, the building was first subdivided into three luxury apartments in the 1930s and housed some of Hollywood's most famous bachelors.

As the years passed, it was divided again and again into smaller units. But traces of the building's glamorous past still lingered—the wrought-iron balconies, the turret, turquoise trim the color of the Pacific, the lush courtyard garden. There was a certain appeal in its faded beauty, as if it represented the golden days of Hollywood, now long gone. But Garrett had little time to reflect on the history of the place he called home as he headed toward his car.

Twenty minutes later, he pulled into his parking spot at the *Post.* He'd been ordered into work by his editor, Don Adler, who had issued the curt invitation via a seven a.m. phone call. Garrett was rarely required to come into the office and meetings were rarely scheduled before ten a.m.

"How could you write something like this?" Adler shouted, waving a folded copy of the *Post.*

"Good morning to you, too," Garrett muttered as he flopped down on Adler's couch. "What's the problem?"

Garrett looked up at his editor and watched him pace back and forth across the width of his office. "The problem? The column is the problem."

"You read it before we went to press. You told me you loved it. My readers loved it."

"I want you to print a retraction."

Garrett laughed. "I will not! My column is humor. You don't print a retraction for humor. What am I supposed to say? The *L.A. Post* regrets the error? This wasn't supposed to be as funny as you thought it was? What has gotten into you?"

"Richard Parker."

"What the hell does Richard Parker have to do with this?"

"What the hell? What the hell, you ask? Where have you been, McCabe? Richard Parker is the president and CEO of Parker Publishing. And Parker Publishing owns this paper—and my ass, if I don't straighten this mess out."

"Don't tell me. Richard Parker's wife is a fan of Emily Taylor."

"No. *He's* a big fan. So big, in fact, that Parker is trying to buy Emily Taylor's magazine. Until you stepped in and screwed everything up, it looked like he had a done deal."

Garrett had serious doubts that anything, or anyone, could get in the way of one of Richard Parker's deals. The man was a mercenary, and master of the slash-and-burn technique of business acquisition. He'd done it with the *Post* five years before and with numerous magazines since then.

Parker would buy a large interest, promising to allow the publication to function as it always had. Then he'd begin to exert the financial pressure. Talented creative people would suddenly find themselves without jobs, morale would slip, circulation would begin to drop, and eventually co-owners would be forced to sell their share of the publication to Parker. Parker would be left with a great, though slightly tarnished, publication, which could easily be redeemed with a few more budget cuts, some indiscriminate terminations and a management staff filled with Parker's henchmen. He now knew exactly where Adler's loyalties were placed. An editor in the pocket of a publisher was a very dangerous thing.

"It's humor, Don. Everyone knows that. And Parker should, too. Can't the woman take a joke?"

"High priestess of herbs and spices? The queen of chintz? A Svengali for the soap opera set? Real funny."

"I think it is. That's why I wrote it."

"I want you to fix this, McCabe. Today. Or you'll be writing obituaries for the next ten years. Emily Taylor means a lot more to Parker Publishing than Garrett McCabe does right now. If you know what's good for your career, you'll make Mr. Parker happy and personally apologize to Ms. Taylor for your unfortunate remarks."

Garrett stood up and leaned across the desk. "You want me to apologize for one of my columns?"

Adler nodded. "Me and Mr. Parker and the rest of the staff at Parker Publishing."

He shook his head. "No way. I'd rather write obituaries. I'll write the funniest damn obits you've ever read. People will buy the *L.A. Post* just to read the death notices."

"McCabe, this is your job on the line here. Don't blow it over some stupid little housewife."

Garrett turned and walked to the door and yanked it open, then looked back. "I can't believe you're siding with Emily Taylor. What happened to the first amendment?"

"There's nothing in the first that guarantees me my job," Don explained. "Or yours, either. Parker signs my paycheck and what Parker wants, Parker gets. Right now, Emily Taylor is the flavor of the day."

Garrett spun away from the door, then cursed beneath his breath as he strode toward his desk. "Alvin!" he shouted. "Alvin, where are you?"

Alvin Armstrong, intern, gofer and all-around whipping boy, came running from the other end of the newsroom. Though Alvin officially belonged to the sports department, most of the reporters there were happy to rid themselves of this perpetual fount of inane sports trivia. The gawky kid, a journalism student at UCLA, wasn't much older than nineteen or twenty, his short-cropped hair and smooth face making him look even younger.

"I prefer *Alex*, Mr. McCabe," he said, forcing his squeaky voice into a more masculine tone. "Alex is a much better name for a sports reporter. Alex Armstrong."

"Alvin, Alex, whatever," Garrett said irritably. "I want you to find a good florist and order a dozen roses. No, make it two dozen, yellow roses."

Alvin smiled crookedly. "Problems with the babes, Mr. McCabe? Hey, I can relate. Women—can't live with them, can't shoot—"

"But before you order the roses," Garrett interrupted, "I want you to track down a woman named Emily Taylor. She's—"

"Oh, I know who Emily Taylor is," Alvin said. "Parker Publishing is negotiating to buy her magazine, *At Home*. Parker's even put her up at his beach house in Malibu. She's doing some work for the magazine while she's here with her partner, Nora Griswold."

Garrett gaped at Alvin. "She's staying at his beach house? How do you know these things? And more importantly, why don't *I* know these things?"

"I've got a friend in the mail room who keeps me informed," he said in a covert tone. "He told me Parker is throwing a big party for her tomorrow night at his place in Beverly Hills. My buddy addressed and delivered the invitations. He snitched one off the top. Engraved. Real fancy."

"They're throwing a party for her? They never threw a party for me."

"Hey, when you meet her, could you get me an autograph? My mom is a megafan. She has all her books. She'd flip if I got Emily's autograph for her."

"My invitation must have gotten lost in the mail," Garrett said dryly.

"That's probably because you blasted her in your column yesterday, huh? You really shredded her bad." Alvin giggled. "The megalomaniac leader of an insidious cult of finger-sandwich fanatics?"

Garrett dragged Alvin into his cubicle. "Can you find out where she is? I mean, right now?"

"Sure. Parker's secretary coordinates her schedule and my buddy's probably seen it. Everything goes through the mail room."

"Great. I want you to buy the roses and deliver them personally." Garrett turned to his desk and grabbed a piece of paper, then scribbled a note. "Dear Ms. Taylor," he muttered to himself as he wrote. "Sorry about the column. Hope you don't take it personally. I certainly didn't. Sincerely, Garrett McCabe."

He shoved the paper into Alvin's hand. "Put this in the box. Then come right back here and tell me how it went. Like a good reporter, I want you to observe the situation carefully. Take in all the details."

Alvin held out his hand. "I need bus fare and money for the flowers."

Garrett reached into his pocket and pulled out his car keys. "One scratch, one ding, and I'll wring your little pencil neck. Leave the top up and don't drive on the freeways. I want you to stay ten miles under the speed limit at all times. Got it?"

"Wow!" Alvin cried. "Your Mustang. You're going to let me drive your Mustang?"

"And the *Post* pays for the roses. Take the money out of petty cash. Just get the job done. I've got a column to write and no time to play adoring fan to Ms. Emily Taylor."

Garrett waited until Alvin left, then settled down at his desk and began to brainstorm ideas for his next column. Usually, he wrote at home, but right now he was too keyed up to get much of anything done within a half mile of his couch. Besides, until Alvin got back, he didn't have a car. He stared at the blank CRT and tapped his foot impatiently with the blinking cursor.

But an hour later, the cursor still waited for its first word. Garrett rubbed his eyes. Why bother? He knew he wouldn't be able to write anything in such a foul temper. It felt immensely satisfying to know that the columnist who'd single-handedly helped increase the circulation of the *L.A. Post* among men age twenty-one to thirty-five was now playing second fiddle to a professional homemaker with a frosty attitude.

Maybe it was finally time to make the big break. He'd explored the possibility of leaving the *Post* and striking out on his own, selling his column to dailies all over the country. He'd even contacted a number of syndicates but no one had come up with an offer yet.

A syndicate deal would mean total independence. He could live anywhere he wanted. All he needed to work was a computer and a fax machine. An image of a mountain cabin overlooking a crystal clear lake came to mind and he lost himself in the daydream. It would be the perfect bachelor life, fishing in the morning, writing in the afternoon and reading the classic works of fiction in the evening. In his spare time, the sports channel would provide diversion with whatever game happened to be on.

"Mr. McCabe?"

Garrett snapped back to the present and spun around in his chair. Alvin stood at the entrance to Garrett's cubicle, a squeamish expression suffusing his face. He held a long florist's box.

"What's wrong? Didn't you find her?" Garrett asked.

"I did just what you told me to. Her partner, Ms. Griswold, took the roses to her. A few minutes later she brought them back and sent me away." Alvin pulled the top off the box and dumped the contents on Garrett's desk. Twenty-four stems tumbled out along with twenty-four disconnected blossoms. Tiny scraps of his note fluttered over the ruined roses. Alvin sighed sympathetically. "I've had some experience with the babes, Mr. McCabe, and I'm almost positive this means she doesn't like you."

Garrett picked up a beheaded rose stem, his jaw tight. "She may not like me now, Alvin, but she doesn't really know me, yet. I can be quite charming if given the chance."

2

"THERE'S GOT TO BE a way to get more color in this layout," Emily whispered desperately. "It's so . . . boring."

She stared at the large tabletop in the center of the photo studio, her chin cupped in her hand, her finger tapping against her cheek. She'd spent the last three hours overseeing the precise arrangement of the twenty different types of mushrooms available to consumers in the United States. And now, she wasn't happy with what she saw.

"We're photographing fungus," Nora replied. "They're all brown or gray or white. There's not much more we can do with them except toss a little spaghetti sauce over them and sprinkle on the Parmesan."

"The feature will disappear on the page. Tell Colin I want more color, Nora."

"No," Nora replied stubbornly.

Emily turned to stare at her partner in surprise. Nora raised a haughty brow and crossed her arms over her ample bosom, a move that usually meant she was preparing to dig in her heels. But she'd never dug in with Emily before.

"No?" Emily asked. "You don't think the layout needs more color?"

"Of course I do, but I'm not going to tell Colin. I'm tired of being the bearer of all your bad news. The last time I made a suggestion on a layout, he told me precisely where I could put my seventeen different varieties of winter squash. You tell him."

"But I can't," Emily said. "He's the best food photographer on the West Coast and I'm—well, what do I know about photography, anyway?" She sighed. "Maybe it isn't so bad after all."

"You want the layout changed, Em? Tell him. You're the boss. Just be assertive."

"Assertive," Emily repeated. "There's that word again. I don't understand why you're suddenly so determined to make me into something I'm not."

"Because, I think it's about time *you* get exactly what you want. Stop being content with whatever comes your way, Emily Taylor. You want more color in the layout, tell Colin yourself."

Emily groaned. "This has turned into a personal crusade with you, hasn't it?"

"Emily, we have an opportunity to make *At Home* the biggest thing in the market. But to do that, you have to become a more powerful part of the image. And to do *that*, you have to stop acting like a shrinking violet. So, let's start with something small. Colin. Give it a try."

Emily watched as Colin returned to the studio and adjusted the lighting around the table. Maybe Nora was right. Maybe she should at least attempt to make more of an effort to be an active part of the business side of *At Home*. But was starting with Colin really wise? His photos had graced the pages of their magazine any number of times and she and Nora were lucky to get him. Magazine work paid a fraction of what advertising photography did, and *At Home* paid even less. She certainly didn't want to damage their already tenuous relationship.

Emily muttered a quick affirmation to herself for good measure then cleared her throat. "Colin?" she called softly. The photographer didn't turn around. Emily glanced over at Nora and made a face, but her friend planted her hand in the small of Emily's back and gave her a shove.

She approached the photographer hesitantly. "Colin," she said. "I—I'd like to discuss the layout—of this shot— with you." She drew in a deep breath. "There's not enough color."

Colin glanced over his shoulder, a shiitake pinched between his thumb and forefinger. "What?" he said distractedly.

"There's not enough color," Emily repeated. "In the layout. I'd suggest we use some natural elements. Like moss," she added. "Yes, that's what I'd like. Moss."

He raised a pretentious brow. "Moss?"

She nodded firmly. "Yes. I'd like you to enhance the layout by using things found on the forest floor, the natural habitat for mushrooms, bark, colorful leaves, pretty stones, maybe even some wildflowers or ferns. I think this will add the needed texture and color to the photos. It will make the layout more interesting."

Colin studied her for a long moment and she swallowed convulsively. "Or maybe not," she croaked. What had ever possessed her to speak up? After all, she wasn't a photographer, and here she was, trying to tell one of the best how to do his job.

After an excruciating wait, Colin merely shrugged. "No problem. I'll get right on it."

"You—you will?" Emily asked, a sigh a relief escaping along with her words.

"Of course," Colin said. "You're the boss."

"Well," she breathed. "Yes, I am, aren't I. I—I'm glad you recognize that." She sent a silent prayer of thanks to Dr. Rita and vowed to take her affirmations more seriously from now on. Colin hurried off to give detailed instructions to his team of assistants. Emily turned and sauntered back to Nora. "Are you satisfied now?"

"Perfectly. And how do you feel?"

She held up her fist and crooked her arm, pointing to her bicep. "Tough, powerful, invincible. Like Wonder Woman."

"Good," Nora said. "Now that you're Wonder Woman, we have a little problem I think we'd better discuss before Friday night's party."

Emily groaned as she began to stuff her file folders back into her tote bag. The last thing she wanted to talk about was Richard Parker's party. She didn't feel all that powerful when she tried to picture herself mingling among crowds of publishing bigwigs, frantically trying to think of something clever or erudite to say.

Emily's silent fretting was interrupted by one of Colin's assistants. "Ms. Taylor, there's a Mr. Garrett McCabe here to see you. He said you'd be expecting him."

"Oh, oh," Nora muttered. "The devil now makes house calls."

"The devil?" Emily frowned. "Who's Garrett McCabe? I don't know a Garrett McCabe, do I?"

"Tell Mr. McCabe that Ms. Taylor is too busy to see him," Nora ordered.

"I am?"

"You don't want to see him. Believe me, Emily."

But Colin's assistant didn't have time to carry out Nora's order. An instant later, a man pushed past her and headed toward Emily, the huge bouquet of flowers in his arms obscuring his face. He shoved them at her, whacking her in the face with a white chrysanthemum. "Here," he ordered. "Take these."

For a floral delivery man, she'd never encountered anyone so rude! She shoved the flowers aside and peered through the greenery at a face that seemed strangely familiar. Tall and tanned, he was dressed in a trendy sports jacket and pleated pants. His light brown hair was streaked golden with the sun, and a blue shirt set off his pale eyes. Those eyes watched her coldly and she felt a shiver skitter up her spine. Somehow, she sensed this was no delivery man.

"Do—do I know you?" she asked.

A smile twisted at the corners of his firm mouth. "If you want to play some silly little power game, that's fine with me," he said. "I'm here to officially apologize and if you know what's good for you, you'll accept my apology. That's not a threat, Ms. Taylor, but a suggestion that I'd take seriously if I were you."

"I—I'm afraid I don't understand," Emily stammered, her eyes fixed on his handsome face. She tried to look away, to gather her senses, but it was as if she looked upon a masterpiece, a sculpture of hard, cold marble, an image of masculine perfection suddenly come to life.

"Don't play dumb, Betty Crocker. I know what you're up to and that sweet little homemaker act may impress Richard Parker, but it doesn't wash with me. I can see right through you."

Shocked out of her daydream, Emily's gaze darted down to her plain flowered dress, then at the lighting behind her. See right through her? Oh, Lord, had she forgotten to put on a slip this morning? Her face warmed in embarrassment and she clutched the flowers in front of her. Who was this man? And why was he so angry at her? And why was he commenting on her lack of proper lingerie?

"Mr.—Mr.—"

"McCabe." He laughed harshly. "I've got to admit, you're good. So cool and composed. And I'm just a vague memory to you, is that it?"

"Yes," Emily said. She swallowed hard. If they had met before, why hadn't she remembered? After all, one doesn't meet Greek gods everyday.

The man named McCabe shook his head in disgust. "I give up. I did what I was told but I'm not going any further. I've apologized. But you mess with my career again, Ms. Taylor, and I won't be responsible for my actions. Got it?"

Wide-eyed and unable to speak, Emily nodded mutely. Somehow she knew their conversation was about to end, and that he'd leave as quickly as he'd arrived. She opened her mouth to say something—anything—but she lacked the words to make him stay.

With a muttered curse, the man turned on his heel and stalked to the door, slamming it shut behind him. The air vibrated with tension long after he left. Finally, Emily slowly released the pent-up breath she had been holding. "How did I ever forget meeting him?"

"You were a little distracted," Nora replied with a tight smile. "That's the guy from the bookstore. The one who tried to shake your hand and talk to you. I didn't realize it until now, but I bet he was scoping you out!"

"I guess I should have shook his hand, huh?" The thought of touching all that sheer masculine energy positively frightened her. She drew a shaky breath and pressed her palm to her racing heart, staring at the door he'd slammed just moments before. "He seemed awfully angry over such a simple breach of etiquette. I think I've had my first encounter with a crazed fan." She turned to Nora. "This is exactly why I don't want to be a celebrity."

"I don't think Garrett McCabe is a fan," Nora said. "Though he may very well be crazed." She retrieved her briefcase, withdrew a newspaper clipping, and handed it to Emily. "I think you better read this, Em. I didn't want to show it to you, but it will explain Mr. McCabe's rather bizarre behavior."

Emily shifted the flowers in her arms and scanned the byline, then looked up at Nora in surprise. "He's a newspaper writer?"

"That's also debatable. Read it," Nora ordered.

Slowly, Emily read the words. But as she made her way through the article, her mind couldn't seem to comprehend McCabe's intent. His biting, sarcastic style was probably meant to be humorous, but she didn't find anything laughable about it. He was poking fun at her, at her work, her readers and everything she found important in her life!

In a rush, the past came back, like a slap in the face, and she blinked back the tears that stung at the corners of her eyes. She'd heard this all before . . . so long ago, she'd almost managed to forget. Back then she'd just smiled and accepted it. Eric had belittled everything she took pride in, and she'd actually believed he was right—what she did *wasn't* important.

And now, this Garrett McCabe had appeared, another incarnation of her ex-husband, a devil disguised as a Greek god. But no matter how handsome and charming he might be, he had no right to say these things about her! He didn't even know her. For once, she didn't try to control her anger, to rationalize her reaction. She *had* changed at least a little in the years since her divorce. And she had every right to be angry at this man—and all those other men who refused to acknowledge the value of her work, including her ex-slimeball, as Nora called him. She was good at what she did and her readers deserved respect for making a comfortable home for their families.

"I'm sorry, Em," Nora said. "I thought about showing the article to you, but I knew how much it would hurt you."

"Don't be sorry," Emily said softly, steeling herself against the flood of painful memories that rushed through her mind. "I'm glad I saw it. And I'm not hurt."

"You're not?" Nora asked, hopefully.

"No," Emily said. She silently chanted one of her affirmations then looked at Nora. "I'm—I'm mad. I'm really, really angry."

Nora smiled in relief. "Then you won't mind what I did."

Emily arched a brow. "That depends. What did you do, Nora?"

"The way I see it, Mr. McCabe got into hot water with Richard Parker over his recent column. Our Mr. Parker just happens to own Mr. McCabe's newspaper. Mr. Parker didn't like what he read in Mr. McCabe's column. And as an apology for his unprovoked attack, Mr. McCabe sent you two dozen yellow roses and a very conciliatory note."

"He sent me roses? And a note? When?"

"Earlier this afternoon," Nora explained. "But I knew how you'd feel, that is, if you had read the column in the first place. So I sent the roses back . . . with the heads snipped off . . . and I tore up the note. I'm sorry, but it was that workshop I took on constructive revenge. I couldn't help myself."

A mischievous smile stole over Emily's lips. "Personally, I would have stomped on them and then put them through the paper shredder, first."

Nora chuckled. "So, you're all right with this? I thought you'd choose to accept his apology."

"Please!" Emily cried, schooling her voice into nonchalance. "The high priestess of herbs and spices doesn't lower herself to consort with some self-absorbed Greek god with a superiority complex. I've never held a grudge in my life, but maybe it's time to start."

That might be easier said than done, Emily mused. As the scent of flowers touched her nose, an image of Garrett McCabe drifted through her thoughts. He was an incredibly unforgettable man, handsome, intense and powerful. Her thoughts lingered over the smooth planes and hard angles of his face, his broad shoulders and long legs, his sculpted mouth and pale blue eyes.

Emily sighed. As Nora would say, he was one incredible hunk of manhood. But that didn't change the fact that he was still the enemy.

"LOOK AT THIS! These are the phone logs from the circulation department. Three hundred calls in just one day. A new record! And all of them condemning your column on Emily Taylor."

Garrett stood at the window in his editor's office and stared down at the street from the third floor. What had he gotten himself into? He'd written a humorous column about a public figure, something he'd done hundreds of times before. Suddenly, everyone was treating him as if he'd vilified Mother Teresa.

He turned from the window and walked over to his editor's desk. Adler reached for a bottle of antacid tablets and shook a number into his hand, then popped them in his mouth. He offered the bottle to Garrett but Garrett declined with a shake of his head.

"I want to know what you plan to do about this mess you've created," his editor mumbled through the mouthful of tablets.

"The mess *I've* created? Don't you see what she's doing? She's using this situation to up the ante for the negotiations. She's trying to show Parker how popular and valuable she is. And she's using me and my career to do it. She's probably behind all these calls." Garrett laughed harshly.

"How many of these callers actually subscribe to the *Post?* Has anyone checked?"

Adler smoothed his thinning hair. "Of course we've checked. They all subscribe," he said. "Listen, McCabe, the order's come down from the top. Either you make nice with Ms. Taylor or Parker's going to go looking for a goat. And I personally don't relish a diet of alfalfa and tin cans."

"You're blaming me for this? You read the column, Don. You're the editor. You could have yanked it. *You* didn't know this would happen anymore than I did."

"All right, all right. But did you at least try to apologize?"

"Twice yesterday. Flowers each time. But Emily Taylor is one tough cookie. I don't think she wants to accept any apology from me. Not until she's used this situation for all it's worth."

"There's got to be a way we can make this disappear," Adler said. "Think of something!"

Garrett placed his palms on Adler's desk and leaned over. "Get me an invitation to Parker's party," he said, "and I'll put an end to this skirmish before it escalates into an all-out war. She can't refuse an apology from me in front of half of Parker Publishing *and* Richard Parker."

"You expect me to give you my invitation? No way. My wife would kill me if she didn't get a chance to meet Emily Taylor."

"Emily Taylor," he said disgustedly, slamming his palms down on Adler's desk. "I wish I'd never met the woman." He sighed, then raked his fingers through his hair. True, his life would have been much easier had he never set foot in that bookstore. But somehow, he couldn't make himself regret their meeting.

There was something about Emily Taylor, something so intriguing, yet so contradictory. On the surface, she appeared plain, unalluring, the type of woman who usually wouldn't warrant a second look from him. But he couldn't help feeling an odd attraction to her. Something beneath that unremarkable surface drew his eyes to her face, his ears to the sound of her voice, until he had to physically tear himself away.

Power, that had to be it. Power in such a pretty and innocuous package would pique any man's interest. But Emily Taylor had no idea who she was up against. He was not going to let her win this battle of wits, this struggle for power. Sweet and innocent as she might act, he would expose her for what she really was. A tiger in kitten's clothing.

"Never mind," Garrett muttered, walking to the door. "I don't need your help. I can take care of this problem myself." Then he stopped and shook his head. He had suspected his editor was spineless, but he'd never had to deal with such an unabashed invertebrate before. Parker had certainly chosen his minions well. "You know, Don, I expected at least a little more support from you."

"You have my support, McCabe. One hundred percent. Now get out there and sweet-talk Emily Taylor into calling off her dogs. You do and I'll get you that raise you've been asking for. And neither one of us will have to pose as any barnyard animals in the near future."

Garrett strode out of Adler's office and pulled the door shut behind him. "Alvin!" he shouted. "Alvin, I need you!"

Alvin seemed to appear out of nowhere at his side. Garrett wondered whether he just hovered, waiting for a summons, or whether the guy actually did any work. He always seemed to be available for whatever odious task Garrett assigned to him, any time, day or night. He followed Garrett to his cubicle, hard on his heels.

"Alvin, I want you to get me one of those fancy invitations for Richard Parker's party."

"It's Alex, sir," Alvin said. "I wish you'd try to remember that."

"Right. Alex. Call up your friend in the mail room and see what he can do. There have got to be a few extras lying around." Garrett grabbed his jacket from the back of his chair, then snatched a pencil and a pad of paper from his desk. "Then I want you to bring it over to Flynn's for me."

"Flynn's? Don't you have a deadline?"

"I write better with a beer in my hand. Besides, I have hours until my deadline." He glanced at his watch. "Seven hours to be exact. You can handle this, can't you—"

"Alex," the kid insisted.

"Right. Alex," Garrett repeated distractedly.

"So, you're going to see Emily Taylor again?" Alvin asked, a dopey grin on his face.

"I don't have much choice," Garrett replied. "Not if I want to keep my job."

"I bet she's real pretty," Alvin remarked.

Garrett turned to him in surprise. "What? When have you seen her?"

Alvin flushed red. "I—I haven't. I just imagine that she is. Kind of like my mom. Only much younger . . . and prettier . . . and nicer. Is she?"

"I don't know your mother," Garrett said. "But I'd be willing to bet that you wouldn't want Emily Taylor running your life."

With that, Garrett headed through the newsroom and took the back stairs to the parking lot. He pulled the Mustang out onto the street and settled in for the drive from downtown L.A. to his favorite hangout. Wilshire Boulevard was clogged with traffic going west, making the three-mile drive less than relaxing.

His thoughts drifted to Emily Taylor, the huge bouquet of flowers clutched in her arms, her green eyes staring at him in mock bewilderment, perfect features schooled into a shocked expression. On the surface, she didn't have the look of a cold, ruthless businesswoman. In fact, she was rather pretty in a simple, unadorned way, soft and sweet.

Garrett shook his head in disgust. Somehow, she'd contrived to maintain a deceptive facade, a wide-eyed innocence that belied the barracuda beneath, so effectively that even he had been fooled. No doubt she worked hard to convey the happy homemaker image for her readers.

Yet, no matter how much he tried to believe the worst, there was still something strangely enigmatic about Emily Taylor, as if she were holding back some secret part of her, hiding something she didn't want the public to see. Maybe that was what attracted him to her, a writer's natural curiosity for the unknown.

Flynn's was busy with the after-work crowd when he arrived. He recognized Jill Foyle, his neighbor at the Bachelor Arms, sitting at the end of the bar. She was chatting with Eddie Cassidy, Flynn's bartender and also a member of the Tuesday night poker group.

Garrett slid onto the empty stool next to Jill and tossed his pencil and pad on the bar. "Ms. Foyle," he teased. "What's new on the singles scene?"

Jill turned to him, tucked her salon blond hair behind her ear and smiled wryly. "What's wrong, McCabe? Stuck for a story idea again?"

Divorced from her computer salesman husband, Jill had moved to L.A. from Boston to start a new life in a warm weather paradise. She was in her early forties, though she looked younger. Jill was incredibly sexy, but he had decided long ago that she was much too good a friend to consider dating. Everyone in the building adored Jill and she returned the feelings in full measure.

"You're on top of all the trends, Foyle. You gave me chocolate as an aphrodisiac. You gave me the inside story on on-line computer dating. Do you have something hot or not?"

"Not," Jill replied. "After you blasted poor Emily Taylor in your last column, I'm not sure I want to be seen associating with your kind. We interior designers consider her one of our own."

Garrett groaned. "Not you, too."

Eddie handed Garrett a cold bottle of beer and a glass. "Kim was all bent out of shape about that column, too," he said. "She called you a pig. You really ripped on her, McCabe."

"That was the whole point," Garrett said. "People seem to forget that I write humor for a predominantly male audience. Didn't you think it was funny, Eddie?"

"I thought it was hilarious. And you hit it right on the head. Sometimes I feel like Emily lives with us. It's Emily this and Emily that. Kim's always got one project or another going and I'm usually the one who has to help her fix whatever decorating disaster she starts. She doesn't like to read directions."

"Emily's projects are always very simple and very tasteful," Jill said. "I've done a few of them myself. She gives great decorating advice to people who might not be able to hire a professional designer. And I'm all for good taste, no matter where it comes from." She gave Garrett a meaningful look.

"You don't think my column was in good taste?"

Jill patted him on the arm. "You may find this hard to believe, McCabe, but I thought it was chauvinistic...

boorish . . . and narrow-minded. Not that that's anything out of the ordinary for you, but I didn't like your choice of targets this time."

Garrett held up his hand. "All right. How was I to know that the woman is considered a saint?" He took a long swallow of his beer. "Our Lady of the Stubborn Bathtub Ring," he muttered.

"She *is* a saint. She's made it fashionable to be a homemaker, again," Jill said. "Is it any wonder she has legions of fans?"

"I'm not one of them," Garrett said.

Jill laughed. "Just what is your big problem with Emily Taylor?"

"Covert domestication," Garrett said. "She and her army of housewives are trying to turn all us men into house pets. Emily Taylor seems obsessed with transforming a man's castle into a—a woman's castle."

"Did you ever think these men might enjoy the homes their wives have made for them?" Jill asked. "Who knows, even *you* might enjoy coming home to a well-cooked meal and a nicely decorated house . . . and a wife who doesn't think you're a raging egomaniac."

Garrett feigned a look of shock. "I *have* a nice home and good meals. And there's no one telling me to pick up my socks or take out the garbage."

"Take-out burritos and a beat-up recliner is not a life," Jill replied.

"Tru Hallihan gave me that chair. *His* wife wouldn't have it in the house. And there's a perfect example of what I'm talking about."

"Do tell," Jill chided. "How is your recliner a perfect example of anything but bad decorating taste?"

"Tell *me*, Ms. Interior Designer, how many times have you relegated some poor soul's recliner and big screen TV to a damp, musty corner in the basement? How many times have you torn apart a man's workshop and replaced it with a deluxe laundry room and twelve-cycle appliances? Not all of us want to live with ruffles and lace."

"I happen to abhor ruffles and I only do lace when it's absolutely necessary," Jill said. "You know, McCabe, someday you're going to meet a woman who's going to knock your socks off. And when that day comes, you're going to be happy to give her any little thing she wants. Including ruffles and lace."

"Not a chance," Garrett said.

"Look at your two buddies. You can't tell me that Josh and Tru are miserable. The last time I saw them in here they looked positively blissful."

Garrett had to admit that she was right. "Tru and Josh just managed to stumble upon the last two exciting women in all of California," he said. "Except for you, of course."

"You are such a charmer, McCabe." She took a sip of her Brandy Alexander, Jill's regular drink. "So, you're looking for someone exciting?"

"You won't catch me looking for my own personal Emily Taylor any time soon, I can tell you that," Garrett said. "Besides, who'd bother to read a column about bachelorhood written by a married man? Right now, all I'm really looking for is a good story idea."

Jill slipped off her bar stool and picked up her purse from the bar. "Well, I can't help you there. I'm all tapped out, McCabe. You'll just have to handle this one on your own."

Garrett watched her walk out the door, then motioned to Eddie for another beer. Eddie glanced down at the empty pad of paper in front of Garrett. "So, what have you decided on?" Eddie asked. "Who are you going to skewer in your next column?"

"I'd like to go another round with Emily Taylor," Garrett muttered. "Unfortunately, my editor doesn't share my enthusiasm for the subject."

"Haven't you had enough?"

Garrett drew a deep breath. "Not yet." He still had a score to settle with Ms. Taylor and an apology to make. The thought rankled. He'd never backed off a subject in his life. But Emily Taylor wasn't his typical subject. She had Richard Parker and the power of Parker Publishing standing squarely behind her. And if he knew what was good for him, he'd make amends and get on with his career.

The trouble was, Garrett McCabe rarely paid attention to what was good for him.

"IF YOU'RE SO DETERMINED to socialize with the houseplants all night, you really should have worn camouflage instead of your black dress."

Emily glanced up at Nora from the upholstered settee and let go of the foliage she was hiding behind. "I was just admiring this schefflera. It's quite healthy."

Everything surrounding Richard Parker was well cared for—his house, his cars, his wife—and Richard Parker himself. The publisher was the picture of California success with the look of a man who had an army of others to tend to his appearance. Beside him, Emily felt positively rumpled. Her hair refused to stay within the confines of the knot at the nape of her neck. Her dress was a size too big. And her panty hose had a run working its way up from her ankle to her knee.

Emily looked at her elegant surroundings. What could he possibly want with her little magazine? He had everything already—a huge Beverly Hills mansion, a beach house at Malibu, expensive cars. She could fit her little Cape Cod cottage inside his Beverly Hills home at least three or four times over. And there wasn't a single Emily Taylor project in sight. From the look of her home, the elegant Mrs. Parker didn't believe in do-it-yourself.

"You're not mingling," Nora said in a singsong voice.

Emily leaned back against the wall and moaned. "Why am I here?" she demanded. "Tell me again."

"To schmooze with the powers that be. To chitchat with Richard Parker and his corporate cronies. And to convince them that buying *At Home* is the best idea they've had in years."

"I'm not sure it is the best idea," Emily murmured. Her gaze darted around the room. How could she be sure? Most of what these people had to say to her went in one ear and out the other. Demographics and audits and circulation breakdowns. From the beginning, Nora had taken care of the business side and Emily handled the creative, that was their arrangement.

Still, every iota of her considerably limited business acumen told her that this deal might mean big changes for *At Home*... and Emily Taylor. "They told me they wanted to boost my Q rating and improve my familiarity score. I didn't even know I had a Q rating."

"You don't," Nora replied. "Not yet. But you will. Once we start putting you on the cover every month."

Emily shook her head. "Oh, no. You can forget that idea right now."

"Why, Em?"

"Look at me. Who'd buy a magazine with my hair on the cover? And if you put my picture on the front of the magazine, everyone will know who I am."

"That's the point," Nora said.

"People will recognize me wherever I go. They'll expect me to talk to them in the supermarket. Crazed fans will start stalking me," Emily said. "Like that Garrett person."

"Speaking of fans," Nora said, her gaze wandering over the crowd.

"I know," Emily said excitedly. "Did you see the antique ceiling fans in the garden room? We should really do a feature on—"

"Forget work!" Nora ordered as she tipped her eyeglasses up to peer through them. "I'm talking about Garrett McCabe. He just walked in."

Emily followed the direction of Nora's look then jumped to her feet, her heart suddenly in her throat. She watched him slowly make his way through the foyer. "Oh, dear," she breathed, her eyes fixed on his face. "You don't think he's here to cause trouble, do you?" She craned her neck to see him better, then scolded herself for such a traitorous action. He was the enemy! And she'd do well not to forget that fact. "He's not carrying any flowers. Maybe he doesn't know I'm here."

Nora shot her a impatient glare. "Em, the party is being thrown in your honor."

Emily twisted her hands in front of her. "Then he *does* know I'm here," she said. "I have to find a place to hide. I'll—I'll be in the kitchen. Come and get me when he leaves."

"But this is your party. You don't . . ."

Emily didn't wait around to hear Nora's pleas. She had never been good at confrontation and she suspected Garrett McCabe was at the party for exactly that reason. Whatever ill will he held toward her, she certainly didn't deserve it. And whatever attraction she had toward him was entirely inappropriate. *He* was the one who had insulted *her.* And she certainly didn't need any more of his "apologies."

Emily caught up with a uniformed waiter and followed him toward the back of the house. The kitchen was huge, swarming with caterers and waiters, an easy place to get lost. She watched the activity for a short time then slowly sidled over to a counter where a tray of mushroom caps waited to be stuffed. She picked up a bowl of oyster stuffing and began to drop a dollop in each cap, trying to calm her nerves the best way she knew how—by cooking.

"May I ask what you're doing with my mushrooms?"

Emily glanced up to see a young woman in a chef's apron watching her suspiciously. "I—I just thought I'd help," she said. "Do you have any chopped walnuts? Chopped walnuts would be a wonderful topping for the stuffed mushrooms. The texture would be perfect and that nutty taste really sets off the oysters."

"Walnuts?" The caterer glanced down at the mushrooms and back at Emily, then scratched her chin. "Hmm, walnuts. I never thought of that. Louis!" she shouted. "Find me some walnuts. Now!"

When the nuts arrived, Emily sprinkled some on top and handed a sample to the caterer. The woman's eyes widened as she savored the enhanced taste. "This is good!" she cried. "Very good!"

Emily shrugged, never comfortable with a compliment. "I'm afraid it adds to the calorie and fat content, but I think it's worth it, don't you?"

The woman nodded, then grabbed a skewer of shrimp from a baking sheet. "Here, try one of these."

Emily popped a grilled shrimp into her mouth and smiled. "Wonderful. Lime juice in the marinade, right?"

"How did you know? It's an Emily Taylor recipe," the caterer explained. "She's the guest of honor tonight. Do you think she'll recognize it?"

Emily coughed as the shrimp lodged in her throat. "I—I think so."

"You know, it's really nerve-racking cooking for someone like Emily Taylor. She's got such a reputation for being a perfectionist. And her presentation is always impeccable. Her standards are hard to live up to."

"I wouldn't worry," Emily said softly. "Everything looks and tastes wonder—"

At that instant, the kitchen door swung inward. A waiter shouted as his tray of hors d'oeuvres was knocked right out of his hands and sent flying through the air. It crashed to the floor near Emily's feet, spattering bits of pesto sauce and garlic toast on her legs. She recognized the recipe immediately.

Emily forced her gaze upward, past the intruder's long legs clad in perfectly pressed khakis, past his wide chest and crisp white shirt, his broad shoulders and soft, woven sport coat. Her gaze stopped on the face of her very own personal crazed fan.

Garrett McCabe smiled sardonically. "Ms. Taylor. And where else but in the kitchen."

The caterer gaped at Emily as if Julia Child herself had just materialized out of thin air. "You're—" She lowered her voice to a softer whisper. "Emily Taylor?" She grabbed Emily's hand and shook it so hard Emily was certain she'd never whisk eggs whites to soft peaks again. "Oh, my! We're making your grilled shrimp teriyaki!"

Emily disengaged her hand. "I know." She waved the skewer she still held.

"But, shouldn't you be out there, instead of in here?" the caterer asked. "This party is for you."

"Yes, Ms. Taylor," McCabe said. "What are you doing in here? Not hiding from me, I hope."

She stared at him, voiceless. He looked incredible. Garrett McCabe possessed a casual elegance that seemed to make him even more intimidating. Slowly, he approached. She backed away until she bumped against the counter. In a futile gesture of defiance, she held the skewer of shrimp in front of her like a makeshift sword. But Garrett McCabe took no notice of her weapon. She watched in dismay as he stepped up to her and plucked a shrimp off the end, then popped it in his mouth.

"Umm," he said. "Very good."

"It—it's the lime," she murmured, unable to think of another reply. "In the marinade."

McCabe raised a brow in surprise.

Even his eyebrows were perfect, she mused, studying his forehead for a long moment. Her gaze shifted to his eyes and her idle contemplation came to an abrupt end. "Really," she blurted out. "It's the lime. The recipe is quite simple. The key is not to overcook the shrimp."

This comment caused a confused frown to cross McCabe's face.

"I know, I know, cooking shrimp can be tricky," Emily explained. "Too long and it gets tough, not enough and it's raw."

"She's right," the caterer chimed in. "It took me a long time to master shrimp."

Garrett turned and gave the woman a patronizing glare. "Would you excuse us, please? We have a private matter to discuss."

"I—I can give you the recipe if you'd like," Emily said as she watched the caterer take her leave.

"What the hell are we talking about?" McCabe snapped. "I didn't come in here to get your recipe for shrimp. I came here to settle this little battle raging between us once and for all."

"Battle?" Emily repeated. "Mr.—" Suddenly, as she looked up into his pale blue eyes, she couldn't remember his name. All she knew was that he had the most mesmerizing eyes she'd ever seen. And those eyes now stared directly into hers, making her pulse quicken and her cheeks warm. She felt as if she just stuck her head inside a 400 degree oven.

"McCabe," he growled, grabbing her hand. "Come with me. We have some business to care of. Now."

"I think I'd rather stay in here, if you don't mind. I have some mushroom caps to stuff."

"I do mind." With that, he dragged her out of the kitchen and back into the midst of the party. The crowd parted like the Red Sea as they made their way to the center of the room. Emily felt a flush of embarrassment surge through her cheeks. Everyone had turned to watch them! Garrett McCabe was creating a spectacle. And Emily Taylor made it a point never, ever to participate in a spectacle.

Richard Parker spotted the commotion and crossed the room to stand beside Emily. "Is everything all right, Ms. Taylor?" His voice was filled with concern.

She nodded frantically. "Yes. I—I think so."

Parker turned to the man beside her. "What are you doing here, McCabe? I don't remember inviting you."

"I came here to formally apologize to Emily Taylor for the content of my recent column," McCabe replied.

Parker considered his explanation, then nodded. "Fine idea, McCabe. I knew you'd understand my position in this matter."

Garrett turned to Emily. "Ms. Taylor, I'm sorry if my humor in any way reflected badly on Parker Publishing and the *L.A. Post.* Any slight was unintentional."

"I—I understand," Emily said. "I—I mean, I accept—your apology. Can I go now?"

"And a fine apology it was," Parker said, clapping Garrett on the shoulder. "I'm glad to see that you two are friends now. Ms. Taylor, Mr. McCabe is at your disposal. If you need or want anything during your stay with us, I want you to call McCabe. He'll take care of it. He knows L.A. better than anyone on our staff, so you'll be in good hands. Won't she, McCabe?"

Garrett's expression froze and he turned back to Parker, a look of utter disbelief in his eyes. "I'm afraid I don't have time to—"

"Of course you do. Doesn't he, Adler?"

A balding man at the edge of the crowd nodded. Emily hadn't a clue who Adler was, but he obviously held at least some power over Garrett McCabe, though not nearly as much as Richard Parker.

Parker smiled. "Good. You've got your orders, McCabe. And maybe a little time with Ms. Taylor will give you a chance to see the error of your ways."

McCabe smiled tightly. "Of course. I'd appreciate that. Now if you'll excuse me, Richard, the guest of honor and I have some scheduling matters to discuss."

Emily shot Garrett McCabe a quick glance, then looked down at her pesto-coated shoes. By the furious expression on his face, she wasn't sure she wanted to spend another second discussing any subject with Garrett McCabe.

3

GARRETT GRABBED Emily's elbow and steered her out of the crowded room, past the stares and the whispered words, through the French doors and out onto the huge terrace that overlooked the Parker's backyard. With every step, he made a conscious attempt to control his temper. "I hope you're satisfied," he muttered.

Emily stopped short, tugged her elbow out of his grasp, and took a shaky breath. "I don't understand why you're so angry with me. If anyone should be angry, Mr. McCabe, it should be me." She paused, as if trying to gather her thoughts. "In—in fact, upon further consideration, I *am* angry with you. You said some very unflattering things about me in your column." She stepped away, retreating to the railing at the edge of the terrace.

Garrett shook his head. This woman was something else! She'd refined her righteous indignation right down to the quiver in her sweet voice and the flush in her pretty cheeks. "Give me a break," he muttered.

"It's true," she said from a safe distance. "I don't usually get angry. I'm a very even-tempered person. But some of the things you wrote really got me…miffed." She stiffened her spine and wagged the skewer of shrimp at him like a scolding schoolmarm.

A sharp laugh burst from his throat. Garrett stepped up to her and grabbed the shrimp, then tossed it over the edge of the terrace. "Miffed? Now, that's a polite way to put it."

She looked over the railing as the shrimp dropped to the lawn below. "I—I'm sure you understand my feelings," Emily continued. "No one has ever said such nasty things about me. Except maybe one other person, but that was a long time ago and I'd prefer not to think about that."

Garrett leaned back against the terrace railing and studied her profile shrewdly. "Do you really expect me to fall for this innocent act? I know what you're up to, Ms. Taylor."

"You do?" she asked, risking a sideways glance at him.

"Yes, I do." He smiled in satisfaction. Finally, an opening. Maybe she'd admit that she'd been jerking him around this whole time. She must sense that her act was wearing a little thin.

"What is it, then?" Emily asked.

Garrett frowned. "What is what?"

"What is it that I'm up to?"

He growled in frustration. "Stop it! You can play these games all night long, but it won't change anything. I've got your number, Ms. Taylor."

"Good," Emily said, pushing away from the railing. "Then you can call me tomorrow and we'll discuss this over the phone. You seem to be quite upset and I don't deal well with confrontation. Nora says I should take a class, but I think I'm just a little—" She stopped abruptly as if she just realized she was babbling. "Shy," she muttered, a scowl suddenly marring her perfect features.

Garrett circled her, pacing restlessly. "For someone who's shy, you sure talk a lot."

"I usually don't talk this much," Emily assured him.

"You don't talk, you don't get angry." He paced for a few moments more, then stopped and sighed deeply. "And you don't have a clue, do you?"

"A clue?"

"You don't know why I'm . . . miffed."

"Nora told me that you might be in trouble with Mr. Parker because of what you wrote in your column. But certainly, you can't blame me for something *you* wrote. I didn't ask to be the subject of your column."

Garrett bit back a curse. When she stated it in such a simple way, he was forced to admit that she might be right. After all, he was the one who fired the first shot. She was simply defending herself the best way she knew how. Considering *that* fact, he was acting like a certified jackass. "That's not the point," he said calmly.

"But I told Mr. Parker earlier that I wasn't angry about the column and that it wouldn't affect our business negotiations. After all, freedom of speech is part of the Constitution—or the Declaration, I can never remember which. Either way, I'm as patriotic as the next person."

Garrett studied her as she spoke. On the surface, she seemed totally incapable of guile or artifice. "So, you're not angry?"

"Oh, no. I'm still angry about what you wrote, but I thought it was best to tell Mr. Parker otherwise. He seemed quite worried and I didn't want him to fuss over me."

"You didn't want him to *fuss* over you? But what about the calls to the *Post*? You didn't arrange those?"

"What calls?"

McCabe took a deep breath. He was getting the distinct feeling that maybe, just maybe, he might have misread the situation—and Ms. Emily Taylor. "You're not using this whole incident as a ploy to get a better price for your magazine?"

"I haven't decided whether to sell the magazine to Mr. Parker in the first place," Emily said. "Nora wants to sell, though."

"Nora?"

"Nora Griswold. My partner. She's the one who snipped your roses apart and tore up your note. But I'm certain she did that because she thought she was protecting me, not for some ulterior motive."

Garrett stared at her. Could she really be as sweet and naive as she appeared? No one was *that* sweet, not even his eighty-year-old Granny McCabe. Emily Taylor was a rising star in the publishing field, a savvy businesswoman who'd turned a simple idea into a circulation base worthy of Richard Parker's attention. There *had* to be barracuda blood pumping through those veins of hers. Surely, she only played at being a happy homemaker.

Still, the more he talked to her, the more he began to realize that she was not the person he'd assumed her to be. There was something in those huge green eyes, an openness tempered with a tiny glint of apprehension, as if she were unsure of herself . . . or frightened of him.

"Then my big apology wasn't necessary?" Garrett asked. "I made a fool out of myself in front of my publisher for nothing?"

"Yes," Emily replied, then smiled in embarrassment. "I mean, no. I feel much better about the whole misunderstanding already. And—and I'm glad that you'll be available to drive me around Los Angeles. Nora is a terrible driver. I think it all started with that defensive driving class she took. She keeps confusing that class with her channeled aggression class and I—"

"You don't really expect me to play chauffeur, do you?"

Emily blinked in surprise. "But isn't that what Mr. Parker told you to do?"

"Ms. Taylor," he interrupted. "I have neither the time nor the interest in playing tour guide for you. And let's get another thing clear right from the start—my column was not a misunderstanding or a mistake. I write what I see and I stand behind it one hundred percent."

"But—but you don't even know me!" Emily cried.

"I know enough," Garrett said.

She watched him, her bottom lip trembling slightly. Somehow, he sensed that her emotion was genuine, that she was disappointed in him, hurt and confused by his casual disregard for her feelings. "And I know you," she said softly. "You're arrogant and domineering and close-minded." She paused as if she were through, but then went on. "And you don't know me from—from a melon baller. Your column just proves it."

He wanted to challenge her accusations, but he stopped himself. What did he care what Emily Taylor thought of him? Her opinion should mean nothing to him, but it did. Suddenly, he wanted her to know that he hadn't meant to hurt her with his column. "All right," Garrett said resignedly. "Who are you, Ms. Taylor?"

"Why don't you take the time to find out?" Emily suggested. "I think once you see what I do, you'll realize how wrong you were. Just because I'm a homemaker, doesn't mean what I do isn't valuable. Spend some time working with me and I'll—"

"You'll let me write another column about you," Garrett said with a grin.

"No!" Emily said.

"Then what?" Garrett countered.

She shot a leery glance in his direction. "Then *I'll* consider changing my opinion about *you*."

Garrett smiled. "I guess that's fair enough. I've always considered myself an open-minded person."

"All right," Emily said. "We have a deal, then. And if you change your opinion, you'll print an apology to my readers."

He laughed. "Not a chance, Ms. Taylor. Let's just say I'll make an attempt to understand your side of the story and leave it at that. Is it a deal?"

"All right," she acquiesced.

He held out his hand and she tentatively placed her fingers in his. He glanced down at the short-cropped nails and delicate, tapered fingers. The women he usually dated had long, vividly painted nails, a feature he'd always found incredibly sexy. But there was something quite different about Emily Taylor... and her hands.

He couldn't deny the glimmer of attraction he felt as he touched her. She was soft and sweet and she smelled like fresh air. Emily was a real woman, not some trainer-toned, salon-designed California goddess. She didn't dress provocatively, didn't flirt shamelessly, and seemed totally unaware of her beauty. Her figure wasn't perfect and her hair looked as if she'd styled it with a garden rake. Though she wasn't really his type, he had to admit, her husband probably considered himself a very lucky man.

Her husband. The glimmer faded and Garrett withdrew his hand. "You can reach me at the *Post*," he said. The imprint of her warm fingers still remained. He stuck his hand in his pocket. "Goodbye, Ms. Taylor." He walked to the terrace steps.

"Mr. McCabe?"

Garrett turned back to her. "Yes, Ms. Taylor."

"W-would you mind driving me home?"

At first Garrett was taken aback by her odd request. From anyone else he would have considered it a come-on, but from Emily Taylor it sounded like a desperate plea for help. "Shouldn't you stay?" he asked. "After all, you are the guest of honor."

Emily bit her bottom lip and looked back into the house through the French doors, then shrugged. "I don't want to go back in there. Besides, I don't think they'll miss me. Nora's there and she can answer their questions." She smiled winsomely, her cheeks flushing pink. "All these people make me . . . nervous. I'd much rather go home but Nora has the car keys."

Garrett chuckled then held out his hand. When she stepped to his side, he tucked her fingers into the crook of her arm, then led her down the terrace steps. "Maybe you were right, Ms. Taylor."

"About what?" she said, looking up at him with those incredible eyes.

"Maybe I don't know you from a—what was it again?"

"Melon baller," she said, blushing prettily.

THE TWENTY-MILE DRIVE to the beach house in Malibu passed in near silence. Emily had never been adept at small talk—unless it involved the proper way to separate an egg or the merits of aluminum cookware versus copper. She was nearly certain that Garrett McCabe wouldn't be interested in her opinion on pots and pans, or eggs for that matter.

So they listened to the car radio, a soft rock station that Garrett hummed along with every now and then. He had a nice voice, deep and rich and warm, and she closed her eyes and listened to the seductive sound.

An image swirled in her mind and she saw herself dancing with the tall, handsome man. He was dressed in a tuxedo and she was dressed in a long, white evening gown— store-bought, not one she'd sewn herself. He held her close, his arm molding her body to his, his breath soft at her ear. He sang along with the music and she smiled, then drew back to look into his eyes . . . pale eyes. She reached up to run her fingers through his sun-streaked hair. . . .

"Emily?"

Emily snapped out of her fantasy with a start and looked over at Garrett. She brought her fingers to her lips. They still quirked in an involuntary smile. To her relief, Garrett hadn't noticed her brief lapse into lunacy. Instead, he stared out the windshield, squinting to read the house numbers in the dark. "Which one is it?" he asked.

She pointed. "Three houses down from the street light."

Garrett smoothly swung the car into the beach house driveway, then turned off the ignition and gazed up at the house. "So, this is what my readers pay for."

"Yes," she breathed.

"Pretty nice."

They sat in silence for a long moment. Then Emily cursed her sudden lack of manners. "Would you like to come in?" she asked. "I—I baked a pie earlier today. And I made some vanilla ice cream." She stifled a groan.

Could she be any more unoriginal? Pie and ice cream? Garrett McCabe was probably used to sophisticated women who always knew the right thing to say. A drink, that's the invitation that would have been more appropriate! A nightcap, wasn't that what it was called?

How could she possibly know the proper etiquette in his situation? It wasn't as if she'd been *out* of circulation for the past eleven years—she'd never even been *in* circulation. She'd married Eric the summer after she'd graduated from high school. He'd been the only man she'd ever dated, the only man she'd ever slept with, and the only man who'd ever driven her home.

At age thirty-four, she'd kissed fewer men than the average high school cheerleader. A grand total of one in her entire life. And though she read a lot of books and saw a good number of movies, neither had prepared her for sitting in a parked car, alone, with a real, live man.

What was she supposed to do? What did today's women usually do at the end of a date? Emily stifled a moan at the possibilities that ran rampant through her mind.

But this wasn't a date, she realized, greatly relieved. So why did she feel compelled to invite Garrett McCabe in? Professional courtesy, she rationalized. But she hadn't said a word to him the entire drive to Malibu. What made her think being alone, in a romantic beach house, with a gorgeous hunk, would suddenly turn her into a brilliant conversationalist? "You don't have to," Emily murmured. "You're probably tired and want to—"

"Sure, I'll come in," Garrett said. "I'd like to get a look at Parker's little home away from home. This is probably the closest I'll ever get to a Malibu beach house."

Garrett hopped out of the car and came around to Emily's side to open her door. He held out his hand. Mrs. McCabe had obviously instilled a proper set of manners in her son. A pity his manners hadn't extended to his newspaper column. He helped her out of the car then fell into step behind her as she navigated the narrow walkway to the door.

Emily unlocked the door and walked inside, then reached for the light switch. With one flip of the switch, the great room filled with light. Fans whirred softly from the vaulted ceiling, lofted two stories high. The night sky was visible through the huge skylights, and even with the windows closed, the sound of the ocean could be heard inside.

"Wow," Garrett said. "This is great."

"It's pleasant enough," Emily said, leading him to the kitchen.

"Don't you like it?"

"It's not home," she replied wistfully. "I feel more comfortable in familiar surroundings."

"If this isn't comfortable, I don't know what is." He sat down on a stool at the counter while she uncovered the pecan pie she'd made earlier. "Where is home?" he asked.

"Rhode Island," she said. "Outside Middletown. That's near Newport. My family had a summer place there. Would you like coffee with your pie?"

"Sure," Garrett said. "I suppose it's hard being away from your family."

"Not really," Emily said. "My parents are very busy with their own lives. My mother does a lot of charity work and my father has his business. And my brothers all have families of their own."

"That's not what I meant," Garrett said. "I was talking about your husband. And your children."

Emily froze, the coffeepot gripped in her hand. "I—I don't have a family," she said softly. "I mean, no children. Do you take your coffee black?"

"Cream," Garrett said distractedly. "Then your husband?"

"No husband, either," Emily replied.

She could sense him watching her, could feel his surprise in the air. "You're not married?" Garrett asked.

She smiled. "I was once, but not anymore. I know it seems a little strange, considering my work. But a home is a home, no matter what combination of people live there. I just happen to live alone. I have flavored coffee," Emily said, anxious to change the subject. "Hazelnut, I think." She looked over at him.

Garrett watched her, his gaze shrewd, an odd smile twisting his lips. "Funny. I just assumed you were married." He slowly pushed up from the stool, his expression suddenly uneasy. He took a deep breath. "Actually, I should get going," he said. "It's a long drive back into the city."

"Of course," she replied. "But let me give you some pie to take home."

"No, that's really not necessary," Garrett said.

"It's no problem," Emily insisted. She grabbed the pie pan, recovered it with tin foil, then handed it to him. "I'd give you some ice cream, but it would be melted by the time you got home."

"Thanks," Garrett said, peeking under the tin foil. "It looks good. Smells good, too."

"I—I hope you enjoy it," Emily said, following him to the door. "It's pecan with bourbon. I can give you the—" She stopped. She was babbling again. "And thanks . . . for the ride."

"No problem," Garrett said, stepping to the door. "See ya."

"See you," she replied as she watched the door close behind him. Her shoulders slumped and she slowly released the breath she was holding. "Stupid," she muttered. "Dumb, dumb, dumb. What is wrong with you, Emily Taylor? The man insults you in a major metropolitan newspaper and you invite him in and give him pie. What would you do for a real enemy, bake him a sponge cake?" She clenched her fists at her side. "I will learn to be more steadfast, I will learn to be more steadfast."

She'd never been able to hold a grudge. Emily Taylor—always so anxious to please and ready to gloss over any conflict, sugarcoat any difference of opinion—couldn't stay angry. Even though she had every right to be angry at Garrett McCabe, maintaining that anger was nearly impossible. Instead, she chose to see the good in him, his impeccable manners, his easy charm, and his handsome features.

With a disgusted sigh, she headed back toward the kitchen. Whenever she was confused or upset, she felt a strange compulsion to bake. She'd bake cookies. That

would make her feel better. But as she creamed the butter
and sifted in the sugar and flour, it took great effort to keep
her mind off of Garrett McCabe and on her recipe.

Two hours and six dozen chocolate chip cookies later, she
felt much better. She'd nearly managed to put Garrett
McCabe out of her mind for good. Until Nora walked into
the kitchen.

"Here you are," Nora cried, throwing her coat on the
counter. "Where did you disappear to? I was worried." Nora
looked around the kitchen, her gaze taking in the cookies,
laid out on brown paper like a platoon of chocolate chip
soldiers. "All right, what's wrong?"

"Nothing," Emily said, straightening a row of cookies.
"You know how I hate parties." As Nora's gaze turned cu-
rious, Emily turned to put the cookie sheet in the sink.

"How did you get home?" Nora asked.

"Garrett McCabe drove me," Emily murmured.

"No wonder you're so upset," Nora said. "What did he
do, tie you up and toss you in the trunk?"

"No. I asked him to drive me."

"Well that was uncharacteristically assertive of you,"
Nora said.

"We had a pleasant drive. He came in, I gave him pie and
he left."

Nora giggled. "You gave him pie? He doesn't seem like the
pie type."

"All men like pie," she explained. "Besides, it was a peace
offering. We've come to an understanding . . . of sorts."

"You're not angry at him anymore, are you?" Nora asked,
clearly a rhetorical inquiry. She shook her head. "How
could you forgive him after he insulted you like that?"

"Oh, I don't know," Emily shot back. She picked up a
cookie and stuffed it in her mouth, then reached for an-

other. "Maybe I'm not meant to be as cranky and obstinate as you are. I'm much better at being nice."

Nora grabbed a third cookie from Emily's hand and tossed it back on the paper. "All right. Tell me about this understanding, Em." She grinned. "I'd sell my soul to have an 'understanding' with a hunk like Garrett McCabe."

Emily felt a blush creep up her cheeks. There were times when she truly believed Nora could read her mind. "It's not like that," she said.

"And why not? Now that you've worked out all your differences, why not see what develops? I bet he's a great kisser."

"I—I'm not interested in getting involved with any man. Especially a man like Garrett McCabe."

"If you waited until you were ready, Em, you'd have to ask for a weekend pass out of the old folk's home."

Emily sighed. "You know I'm no good at relationships. I don't have anything to offer. And I don't ever want to go through what I went through with Eric. Not again. It hurt too much."

"You have plenty to offer," Nora countered. She folded her hands in front of her. "Now, what are your plans for Mr. McCabe? If you're not interested in lust, how about a little revenge?"

"Nora! Give it a rest!"

"I'm just asking. I heard Parker order McCabe to show you around L.A. I was just wondering when your first tour was scheduled. If you don't want to go, I wouldn't mind taking your ticket. I could make him real sorry he ever wrote that column."

Emily reached for the dish detergent. "We haven't made any plans yet. But I've been anxious to visit the Antique Guild." As she filled the sink with hot water, she tipped the soap bottle over and squeezed. "They have three acres of antiques under one roof," she said distractedly, mesmerized by the stream of liquid soap. "I might be able to find something new to add to my bottle collection."

"Em, I think that's enough soap."

Emily looked down to see a huge mound of bubbles pouring over the edge of the sink. With a yelp of surprise, she shut the water off and brushed the bubbles back.

"I can't imagine Garrett McCabe in the midst of three acres of antiques looking for old bottles for your collection," Nora said with more than a hint of sarcasm.

"I really don't care whether he enjoys himself. I just hope this will be a learning experience for him."

"So you *are* interested in revenge," Nora teased.

"I just think if he understood me—I mean, my readers—a little better, he wouldn't be so quick to ridicule. If I could only show him the value and importance of the domestic arts. Making a home in today's world is much more complex than he realizes. It's not just washing clothes and vacuuming the rugs."

"Transference," Nora stated.

"What?"

"I learned about it in a class I took—Freud Made Easy. You're using Garrett McCabe to work through your problems with Eric. If you can prove to Garrett what you couldn't prove to Eric, you'll be able to attain a sense of closure."

"Closure?"

"A proper end. It's sort of like mulching your roses in the fall. You don't want to admit winter is coming and there won't be any more blooms, but once you do the mulching, you accept it. Closure."

"I attained closure the day Eric walked out on me," Emily said.

"Did you?"

She drew a deep breath. "Yes. And I came to a few conclusions about myself at the same time. I'm no good at communicating with men. In fact, I'm no good with men, period."

"You didn't seem to have trouble communicating with Garrett McCabe. I was watching you two out on the terrace."

"He's different. I'm not sure why," Emily said, frowning. "Maybe it's because I was so angry at him. I felt like I had to defend myself."

"Maybe," Nora said, an inscrutable smile curling the corners of her mouth. She picked up a cookie and bit into it. "Or maybe you two are just meant for each other."

"And maybe you should get a life of your own so you'll stop butting into mine," Emily said.

Nora laughed. "My, my, Em. You're positively bursting with assertiveness today. What has gotten into you?"

"Nothing. Except a bad case of exhaustion. I'm going to bed."

Three hours later, Emily was still wide awake, staring at the ceiling of her bedroom and trying valiantly to count sheep. Every inch of her being wanted to drift into slumber. But a strange sense of anticipation fluttered inside her, banishing all possibility of rest. Something had changed, or been set into motion, and though she wasn't sure what it was, she knew she couldn't stop it.

She pulled the covers up over her head. Maybe it was stress over the sale of her magazine. Or maybe she was just tired of Nora's assertiveness lessons. Or maybe it was confusion over her confrontation with Garrett McCabe. Whatever it was, she didn't want to face it.

She just wanted to go home to Rhode Island, where life was easy and unchanging. And where men like Garrett McCabe didn't bother to give her a second glance.

GARRETT PICKED UP the folded note from the floor as he pushed the door to his Bachelor Arms apartment open. Balancing Emily's pie in one hand, he reached for the light switch then kicked the door shut behind him. He leaned back against the door, closed his eyes and slowly released a pent-up breath.

What a day! More precisely, what a night. He wasn't quite sure where everything fell apart. Maybe it was when Emily Taylor told him she was miffed. Or maybe it was when she asked him to take her home. But things were definitely on the downslide by the time she told him she wasn't married.

Whenever it was, it certainly wasn't a moment he'd recall with any great enjoyment. He'd gone from feeling overwhelming anger to undeniable attraction in the space of a single evening. Attraction to Emily Taylor! At first, it was simple to ignore—after all, Emily Taylor, the consummate homemaker, would have to be happily married. But he couldn't deny the unsettling current of pleasure that shot through him when she informed him she wasn't.

Garrett kicked the door again before he crossed the room and flopped down on the couch. What was he thinking? Emily Taylor was the antithesis of everything he usually found attractive in a woman. They had nothing in common. He loved spontaneity, she preferred absolute order. He wrote satire, she wrote recipes. He was a confirmed bachelor and she was a confirmed homebody. He ate fast food and she baked pies.

He pulled the foil off the pie pan and picked up a piece of Emily's pecan pie with his fingers, then took a huge bite. He had to admit, she baked a hell of a pie. He licked his sticky fingers, then unfolded the note. It was a hastily scribbled invitation to Josh and Taryn's place for pizza. With one hand, he crumpled the note and tossed it in the direction of the wastebasket. He didn't feel much like socializing, especially with the happily married set.

But by the time he finished his second piece of pie, he realized that all that waited for him in his quiet apartment was more idle contemplation of Emily Taylor. He pushed up from the couch, washed his sticky hands in the kitchen sink and headed out the door and down the hall. Pecan pie followed by pizza. Not a bad dinner, considering.

At his knock, the door to Josh's apartment swung open. Josh's wife, Taryn, greeted him warmly with a hug and a kiss on the cheek. He'd only known Taryn a few weeks, but she treated him as if she'd known him her whole life. "Garrett! We were hoping you could come up. When did you get in?"

"Just a few minutes ago." Garrett glanced around Josh's apartment—now Josh and Taryn's apartment. He hadn't been inside since Taryn had moved in and was startled at the change. There were canvases everywhere, propped up against the walls, stacked in the corner and hung on every available inch of wall space. But in all the chaos, the apartment finally looked as if someone lived in it. Josh was fastidiously neat, but Taryn had obviously loosened up his penchant for tidiness.

"Josh and Tru went to pick up the pizza," Taryn said. "Would you like something to drink?"

"A beer would be fine," Garrett said as he wandered inside.

"Hi, McCabe," Caroline called from the sofa. She waved and smiled, then patted the cushion next to her.

Garrett sat down next to Tru's wife. He knew Caroline a bit better than Taryn. Caroline's easy familiarity with her husband's buddies had obviously rubbed off on Josh's wife. Garrett found it amazing that they considered him a good friend, simply by virtue of marriage. Taryn handed him a beer, then took the chair across from him.

They silently observed him, like some exotic creature come to visit. "Did you have a date tonight?" Caroline finally asked.

His social life had always been a popular subject with Tru's wife. He served as the marriage counselor's informal research rat on a number of occasions, providing insights into the state of the happily unmarried men in America. "No, I didn't have a date," he said. "Just a business obligation. A party for Emily Taylor."

"Emily Taylor invited you to a party?" Taryn asked, her pale eyes alight with interest. "After your column, I'm surprised she didn't invite you to step in front of a speeding train."

"Contrary to popular belief, Emily Taylor and I get along just fine," Garrett said. "My publisher is trying to buy her magazine so we're going to all be part of the happy Parker family of publishing."

"That's a step in a positive direction," Caroline commented. "Hmm. You and Emily Taylor. It might work. After all, opposites do attract."

Garrett chuckled. "Is that a professional marriage counselor maxim, Dr. Lovelace," he teased, "or one of those old wives' tales?"

"Is he calling you an old wife, Caroline?" Taryn asked.

"Are you calling me an old wife, McCabe?"

"Not a chance," Garrett said. "You're both young, and quite lovely. And if you weren't married to my best friends, I'd marry you both myself . . . if bigamy wasn't against the law."

"And you are too charming for your own good," Caroline said. "So when are *you* going to settle down and get married?"

"I have a good friend I could introduce you to," Taryn said. "Her name is Margaux. She's French and she owns an art gallery. Would you like her number?"

Garrett glanced at his watch and shifted uneasily on the couch. "When did you say Tru and Josh were going to be back?"

"Answer my question, McCabe," Caroline said.

"Yeah, McCabe," Taryn teased. "Answer Caroline's question first. And then answer mine."

Garrett shook his head. "Have you two been talking to my family? They seem to be obsessed with this particular subject as well. Or do you females have some covenant to find a wife for every unattached man?"

Taryn and Caroline glanced at each other and smiled. "We just want you to be happy."

"I *am* happy," Garrett said. "So, you don't have to worry yourselves over my marital status. Can we change the subject?"

"Sure," Taryn said. "Tell us more about Emily Taylor. We're both big fans. What's she like? Did she throw a wonderful party? How was the food?"

"She didn't throw the party, my publisher did. And she's...nice," Garrett said. That was an understatement. She was too nice, if that was possible.

They waited expectantly for more. "That's it?" Taryn said.

"A typically noncommittal McCabe answer," Caroline said. "We know she's nice. She's Emily Taylor. What does she look like?"

Garrett shrugged uneasily. "I don't know. She's pretty, I guess. She's got reddish hair. Curly. About down to here." He put his hand on his shoulder. "Green eyes. She's not too tall. She's got a nice body, curvy in all the right places, but not skinny." Garrett smiled. "And the little woman bakes a heckuva pecan pie."

Caroline clenched her fist and shook it at him. "You are incorrigible."

"It's true. I have some down in my apartment."

Caroline sighed. "I hope some woman finds you soon and teaches you a thing or two before you're a complete loss to society."

At that instant, the door to the apartment swung open. Josh and Tru walked in, each carrying a pizza box. "Hey there, McCabe," Tru said. "Glad you could join us. Did you have a date tonight?"

Garrett shook his head. "It's about time you two got back. This inquisition has been going on far too long. Your wives feel compelled to marry me off like some spinster sister."

"Marriage isn't all that bad, McCabe," Tru said, dropping the pizza box on the coffee table. "You should try it."

"Now there's a glowing recommendation," Caroline said.

Tru turned and smiled at his wife. "You know what I mean."

She returned his smile warmly. "You're lucky I do."

To Garrett's relief, majority rule took over when Tru and Josh returned. The conversation strayed away from matrimony to subjects with more general appeal—an upcoming auto show, a recent monster truck pull, and the basketball playoffs. Usually at the center of any conversation, Garrett chose tonight to sit back and watch the interplay between the two couples. He was amazed at how comfortable his friends seemed in their marriages, how easily they'd made the transition between bachelorhood and married life.

If he'd been asked to lay odds on the potential success of either union before the wedding, the odds would have been long. Caroline and Tru were exact opposites, and Josh and Taryn were even more different, if that was possible. But maybe Caroline was right. Maybe opposites did attract.

He, on the other hand, preferred women who shared his interests and, more specifically, his commitment to the single life. Women who enjoyed the night life and baseball, movies and basketball, fine dining and football. Women who didn't wait around for him to call and didn't care if and when he called late.

But in all his dating life, he'd never had the easy closeness with a woman that he saw between his two friends and their wives. The gentle give and take, the longing looks, the shared smiles, and the deep affection and trust. Suddenly, he felt like a fifth wheel, out of sync and unneeded.

Tru and Josh had something he would probably never have and for the first time in their friendship, he envied them. They had a future with the women they loved, a happily-ever-after. And somehow, his bachelor state paled in comparison. Suddenly, he felt the need to escape, to find a place where he felt comfortable, where he belonged.

Placing his plate on the coffee table, Garrett stood up. "I better be going," he said.

"You don't have to leave already, do you?" Taryn asked.

"Yeah," Garrett said. "I've had a long day. I'll see you guys on Tuesday for poker, right?"

"Tuesday night," Josh said. "See you then."

"Are you sure you don't want Margaux's phone number?" Taryn asked.

Josh turned to her and frowned, then whispered something in her ear.

"I know Garrett is smart enough to get his own dates," Taryn scolded. She turned to Garrett and grinned mischievously. "But Margaux is a very nice woman and I'm sure you'd love her. Did I mention she's French? And she owns a—"

Josh's arm snaked around his wife's shoulder and he covered her mouth with his hand. Garrett gave him a grateful nod as he closed the door on the domestic scene. Halfway back to his apartment, he decided to change course and headed toward the front door. He didn't need peace and quiet. He needed noise and excitement and he knew exactly where to get it.

As he strode through the first floor hallway, he passed the door of apartment 1-G and paused. His mind flashed an image of the mirror and the reflection he had seen there, but he pushed it out of his thoughts and continued on. He didn't believe in ghosts . . . or legends.

There were no empty bar stools at Flynn's when he arrived. The place was loud and smoky and filled with beautiful women. Garrett surveyed the room before he stepped up to the bar. He waved to Eddie and the bartender started toward him.

"Give me a Scotch," Garrett shouted over the din.

"Bad date?" Eddie asked as he placed the glass of amber liquid in front of Garrett.

Garrett stared at the Scotch, then took a swallow. "I'm not sure. I'll let you know after I've had another drink."

He turned his back to the bar and watched as a woman in a tight red dress crossed the room. She sat down at a table with a friend, just as beautiful, in an equally tight dress. On any other day, he would have bought them both a drink and invited himself to sit down. But tonight, he found something slightly distasteful about their provocative appearance.

His mind constantly returned to Emily Taylor, to her winsome smile and her wide-eyed innocence, and her simple, unadorned style. She wasn't pretending to be more than she really was, she wasn't promising something she might not want to deliver.

But even so, he was beginning to believe there might be more to Emily Taylor than he'd discovered so far. He just wasn't sure he wanted to get close enough to find out what it was.

4

"I KNEW I COULD count on you, McCabe. You're a team player and I like that."

Garrett looked across the wide mahogany desk at Richard Parker. He'd been summoned into the publisher's office early that morning by Parker's secretary who had made it quite clear that he had just thirty minutes to appear. He made sure it took him just over thirty-five.

"Team player?" Garrett asked.

"That little apology you made at my party the other night. I couldn't have asked for a better opening. Good instincts, McCabe."

"I don't understand what you're talking about, sir," Garrett replied.

"Let me lay it on the line," Parker said. "We're concerned about Emily Taylor. She isn't convinced that Parker Publishing is the right buyer for her magazine. We want to change her mind and you're going to help."

"Ms. Taylor certainly doesn't trust my opinion on anything," Garrett said, keeping his voice calm and even.

He'd never cared for Richard Parker. The guy was too smooth, too sure of himself, as if his money could buy whatever his greedy little heart desired. Parker had stepped on plenty of people on his way to the top and Garrett didn't relish finding a designer shoe print on his back any time soon.

"Have you seen her since the party last Friday?"

"No," Garrett replied.

"Well, I want you to call her and offer to take her out sight-seeing. Take her to Disneyland or Knott's Berry Farm or any one of those tourist places she wants to see. Spend a lot of money. You can turn it all in on your expense report."

"Personally, I don't think she wants to spend time with me any more than I want to spend time with her," Garrett said.

"Then change her mind," Parker ordered, his practiced warmth suddenly turning icy.

Garrett would not let this man intimidate him. "Why?" he asked blandly.

"Since Emily Taylor has stayed out of the negotiations, it's been hard to gauge her interest," Parker explained, leaning back in his chair and kicking his feet up on the desk. "In order for the sale to be approved, there's got to be a three-way consensus between Nora Griswold, Emily Taylor and Arnie Wilson. Wilson's already given his blessing to the deal. Griswold seems to support our offer, but Emily Taylor is the wild card. If she says no, the deal falls through."

"I don't know how a few sight-seeing trips are going to change her mind," Garrett said.

The publisher took his feet off the desk and leaned forward. "Now that you've smoothed out the situation with that rather misguided column you wrote, I think we might be able to use your . . . talents to further the cause of Parker Publishing." With a restless energy, he pushed out of his huge leather chair and walked over to the window.

"Misguided," Garrett repeated beneath his breath. Another avid supporter of "Boys' Night Out" and the First Amendment checks in.

"Will you look at that?" Parker said, indolently smoothing the sleeve of his designer suit. "Her fan club has been picketing the building all morning. This little battle you've started has turned into an all-out war. We've had letters to the editor, offers for you two to appear on radio talk shows, and Adler told you about the cancelled subscriptions." Parker turned from the window and gave him a shrewd look. "You're lucky the publisher of the *L.A. Post* is behind you one hundred percent." He paused for dramatic effect. "After all, columnists who drive circulation down have a hard time keeping their jobs. At other papers, that is."

Garrett's jaw clenched as he translated the underlying meaning of Parker's words. "But what if she just doesn't want to sell?" he asked.

Parker didn't miss a beat. "Then you'll have to do everything you can to convince her. Look at her, McCabe. She's a divorced housewife from Rhode Island with the business sense of your average gnat. It shouldn't take much of an effort on your part. A little romance would probably go a long way with that one."

Garrett clenched his fists on the arms of his chair. Though he didn't know Emily Taylor very well, he still felt like punching Parker squarely in the nose in her defense. He drew a deep breath and tried to calm his anger. "And if it doesn't?" Garrett asked.

"That's *your* problem, McCabe. She will sell. When she does, we're going to make Emily Taylor a household name. And that name will make a great deal of money for us."

"She doesn't seem to be comfortable with a highly visible public image," Garrett countered. "She told me so."

"This is exactly the kind of information we need, McCabe!" Parker said, clapping his hands. "If she can't play the game, we have to know, so we can make some contingency plans."

"And what might those be?"

"Let's just say that if Emily Taylor isn't willing to take on the role Parker Publishing has in mind for her, we'll deal with her. After all, I'm not buying her, I'm buying her name."

Garrett watched another plastic smile appear on Parker's perfectly tanned face. For all he cared, Parker could take this deal and shove it. Garrett always suspected the guy was a sleaze, but hadn't had any proof until now. Still, he sensed, in this case, it would be best to keep his feelings to himself and play along. Once he found out what Parker was really up to, he could decide what to do.

"What exactly do you want from me, besides serving as Emily Taylor's personal tour guide?" Garrett said.

"Get to know her. Find out what she's thinking. And then guide her in the right direction. Hell, you're the consummate bachelor, McCabe, you know what to do. Give the little lady a reason to move to California."

"And what's in it for me?" Garrett asked.

"Believe me, McCabe, we'll make it worth your while. Let's say, double your salary?"

Garrett schooled his expression and hid his surprise. Double his salary? *At Home* had to mean a lot more to Parker than Garrett had first assumed. At that salary, he'd be making more than his editor.

"So, are you still on the team? Will you help us make this deal work?"

Garrett pasted a smile on his face. "I'll do whatever I can to help," he said, making his lie sound as plausible as he could.

Parker held out his hand and Garrett shook it firmly. "I knew we could count on you. I want you to report back to me on a regular basis. Let me know how Ms. Taylor is doing, any concerns she might have, any stray comments she might make. Just keep her busy, give her an opportunity to open up and confide in you. Turn on the charm, McCabe."

A knot of disgust twisted in his stomach. "That shouldn't be a problem."

"Well, that's that," Parker said, walking to the door and throwing it open. "I'll be looking forward to a successful negotiation and a profitable deal, for both of us."

Garrett stood and slowly strolled to the door. "I'm sure you will," he said. "And I'm sure you'll get everything you deserve, sir." He forced a smile that dissolved from his face the moment he heard the office door close behind him.

Garrett cursed to himself. How the hell did he manage to get himself caught in the middle of this deal? He suspected it was some kind of penance he was paying for attacking the Patron Saint of Pot Roast. He'd rue the day he walked into that bookstore and first set eyes on Emily Taylor. She was the cause of all this....

Or maybe *he* was at fault. Right now, he really didn't care. Under any other circumstances, he'd be ecstatic. A chance to double his salary. But deep down inside, he knew he couldn't endorse any deal with Parker. Garrett didn't trust the man any further than he could spit, so why should Emily Taylor? Not that she'd ever spat in her life.

Garrett couldn't help but feel a strange compulsion to protect Emily Taylor against a guy like that. But if he didn't do as he was told, he'd pay the price. And Parker already had the perfect weapon to use against him—the Emily Taylor column. It wouldn't be hard to fire a columnist who caused so many cancelled subscriptions, never mind the picket line of Emily's readers that had been marching in front of the building all morning.

Garrett didn't wait around for the elevator. Instead, he took the stairs down to the third floor. Shoving against the door to the editorial department, he cursed under his breath.

"Alvin!" he shouted. "Where are you?"

"Over here, Mr. McCabe," a voice sounded from the far side of the room.

Garrett strode to the source of the sound and grabbed Alvin from his cubbyhole in the sports department, dragging him toward Adler's office. The office was empty. His editor could usually be found in the prep room this time of day, supervising the layout of the front page. Garrett pulled the kid inside and closed the door. "I need you to do something for me, Alvin. It's important and you have to keep it completely between the two of us—and your friend in the mail room."

"What is it?" Alvin asked, his eyes wide with curiosity.

"Let's just call it investigative journalism for now," Garrett said. "I want you to talk to your buddy and have him keep his eyes and his ears open. I want to know everything, and I mean everything, that's going on with the *At Home* deal. Any time Emily Taylor's name is mentioned, I want to know about it. A memo goes through the mail room regarding the deal, I want that memo to find its way to the photocopier before it's delivered."

"Wouldn't that be against the rules?" Alvin asked.

"Alvin, sometimes a journalist has to ignore the rules. You have to make a judgment call on what's right and what's wrong. I've had a lot more experience with this than you, so you're going to have to trust me on this one."

"I could get into big trouble."

"If anything happens, it all comes back to me, understand? I'll make sure you're not held responsible, or your buddy, either. Now, do you think you can help me out?"

"I'll try," Alvin said. "But can you to do something for me in return?"

"Anything," Garrett said. "You want to use my car, it's yours. Or you can have my Willie Mays autographed baseball. How about that?"

Alvin shook his head. "Naw, that's okay. What I want is pretty simple."

"Name it," Garrett repeated.

"Can you *please* remember to call me Alex," the kid begged. "Alvin's the name of a chipmunk, not a sports reporter."

Garrett smiled and punched the kid on the shoulder. "Sure, Alex. I think I can remember that. Now, I want you to get to work on our little project. I've got a poker game to go to."

With that, Garrett walked out the office door, leaving Alvin to his investigation. If Parker did have something underhanded in mind for Emily Taylor, he'd have to get by Garrett first.

EMILY STARED DOWN at the photo transparencies on the light table. Any way she looked at them, with or without moss, right side up or upside down, her mushroom feature was as dull as dishwater. Though mushrooms made for wonderful pasta sauce, they made boring photography.

"Interesting shapes," Nora said, peeking over her shoulder.

Emily flipped the light table off. "If that art director you hired sees this, he'll never let me supervise another photo shoot."

"Em, you're the boss. You can do whatever you want, regardless of what Dennis says. That is his name, you know. Not that he minds being known as That Art Director That Nora Hired. But he has worked for us for over three years. You should at least try to remember his name."

"Why? He doesn't like me. Every time I walk into his office, he acts like I'm trying to steal his crayons."

"He's given *At Home* a wonderful look. Without him, Parker Publishing wouldn't have bothered to look twice at our little magazine. And you're just mad because you despise delegating responsibility. You can't do it all, Emily. Maybe in the beginning you could, but the magazine has gotten much too big for that now."

Emily picked up a transparency. "Maybe you're right," she said softly. "So, what do we do?"

"Call Dennis and tell him to work up something new for the next issue."

"But the Varieties feature is mine. I've always done it. I'll just have to find something better, more colorful and exciting. What about pasta?"

"You'd be better off shooting that spread in New York. More Italian markets there," Nora said.

"All right, what does California have that we *can* use?"

"Sand, sun, palm trees, earthquakes, traffic jams. How about movie stars?"

"What about grapes?" Emily asked.

"We're in a veritable fruit and vegetable mecca," Nora said, "but unfortunately, it's spring, not fall. Grapes are harvested in the fall."

"So, what comes in spring?"

"Asparagus. Lettuce." Nora paused. "Lettuce wouldn't be bad."

"And flowers," Emily said. "Lots of flowers. I was reading a brochure on a place called Descanso Gardens. They have over six hundred varieties of camellias. And they have azaleas and spring bulbs and a huge rose garden."

"Our readers don't eat flowers," Nora said.

"Who says 'Varieties' has to be something to eat? You forget, I'm the boss," Emily said. "I can make it whatever I want."

Nora grinned. "I believe I've created a monster."

"Come on, let's go. We'll call to get directions and we can drive over there right now and check it out."

"Em, I've got a lunch meeting with Parker to fill him in on our circulation department and then I've got a teleconference with our advertising reps. I can't go."

Emily's spirits fell. "I guess I could drive out there by myself."

"Or you could call Garrett McCabe. He'd take you."

"I—I don't know," Emily said.

"Come on," Nora said. "Parker said he'd be available to show you around Los Angeles. Come with me and we'll find McCabe down at the *Post*. If he isn't around, you can sit in on the meeting with Parker and we'll drive over to Descanso Gardens after my conference call."

The way she saw it, Emily had three choices and they were all bad. Stay at the photo studio and brood over her mushroom fiasco, sit through a terminally dull meeting with Richard Parker, or get Garrett McCabe to take her to a big flower garden. Maybe starting with a flower garden wouldn't be the best approach to their deal. After all, the way to a man's heart had always been through his stomach, so cooking would probably be a better first lesson.

Not that she wanted to find a way to his heart, of course! Emily stifled a groan. Even though he'd agreed to be her tour guide—under duress—the truth was, she hadn't worked up the courage to take him up on their deal yet. She knew what was holding her back. It was the strange attraction she felt whenever she was near him, and the overwhelming need to prove herself to him, not for the sake of her readers, but for herself. Nora was probably right. What had she called it—transference?

Was she really still living in the past, trying to ease the hurt that Eric's desertion caused? She thought she had moved on, but Garrett's column just seemed to dredge it all up again. The desperate need to please, the unbearable feelings of inadequacy, and the nagging doubt that maybe,

maybe, if she'd just been a little closer to perfect, he wouldn't have left.

But Garrett wasn't her husband, he was a newspaper columnist she barely knew. And she didn't need to prove anything to him if she didn't want to. His column was already history, forgotten by his readers—and hers. Why not take advantage of the offer?

The drive to the *Post* building took only five minutes from the converted warehouse that housed Colin's photo studio. As Nora pulled into the parking ramp across the street, Emily noticed a group of picketers in front of the building. She squinted to read the signs, but it wasn't until she and Nora crossed the street that she could see what the protest was all about.

Garrett McCabe— Dumb as the *Post.*

Homemakers and Proud of It.

Emily Taylor for President.

Emily grabbed Nora's arm and pulled her to a stop. "Oh, no," she murmured. "They *haven't* forgotten yet. Look at that. They're picketing...in support of me. Who told them to come here?"

"No one told them, Em. They're your fans. They're exercising their right to express their opinion."

"But I can't go inside," Emily said. "I can't cross their picket line. It wouldn't be right."

"They won't recognize you," Nora assured her.

"What if some of them were at the book signing? Thanks to you and your brilliant promotional ideas, people know what I look like now. I won't cross that picket line, Nora. It would be an act of treason."

"Then we'll go around to the side door," Nora said. "This isn't a labor strike and you're not a scab. Besides, you can't talk to Garrett McCabe from the middle of the street."

She'd probably be much better off in the middle of the street, Emily mused, among the speeding cars and buses. But she reluctantly conceded the point and followed Nora around the corner to the side door. They wove their way through the first floor of the building which held the prep and press departments and the delivery center. They finally found an elevator and took it to the third-floor editorial departments. When the doors opened, Nora gently pushed her out of the elevator, then continued on to the seventh-floor office of Richard Parker.

"Try to have fun," she called as the doors closed.

The editorial department was a huge, brightly lit room, filled with rows and rows of cubicles and frantic reporters. Emily was sure she'd need a map to find her way through the maze to Garrett's location. She decided to wait at the elevator until someone offered to help her, but after five people hurriedly passed her by without even a glance, she ventured into the thick of the chaos.

Each cubicle was labeled with the name of its occupant, but after searching up and down one row, she decided to ask the next person that she came upon for directions. A skinny young man approached and she forced a smile. She hated talking to strangers.

"Ex-excuse me, I'm looking for Garrett McCabe."

"He's two rows over," the young man said. "I'll take you there."

"Thank you," she murmured. Emily followed him to a cubicle with a sign posted outside. Please Don't Feed the Columnist. Garrett McCabe's nameplate hung beneath it.

"You're lucky you caught him in. He usually doesn't write his column here. Mostly he writes at home. Or at a bar called Flynn's. Have you known him long? I have. He's a real cool guy. By the way, I'm Alex Armstrong, sports." He held out his hand. His voice suddenly seemed lower.

Emily smiled, then sucked in her breath as a figure appeared behind Alex. A smile curved Garrett's firm mouth.

"Well, if it isn't Emily Taylor. Out of the kitchen and into the newsroom."

Alex blinked in surprise at the sound of the deep voice and spun around. "*The* Emily Taylor?" Alex said, his voice cracking, his wide-eyed gaze fixed on Emily. "Wow. My mom loves your magazine. And she's got all your books. Can I have your autograph?"

Emily forced a smile. Even one fan, and a goofy one at that, had the capacity to unnerve her. "Why don't you give me your address and I'll send your mother an autographed copy of my newest book."

"Really? That would be great. My mom will have a cow."

"I hope you mean that figuratively, Armstrong," Garrett said, "because as far as I know, that's not genetically possible."

"I mean, she'll freak. She'll go ballistic."

"That's nice," Emily said, not sure she whether she liked the effect she had on Alex's mom.

"Hey, I'm sorry you didn't like the roses Mr. McCabe sent. He was pretty surprised when I brought them back and they were—"

"Don't you have a job to do, Alvin?" Garrett interrupted.

The boy rolled his eyes and leaned closer to Garrett. "Alex," he said beneath his breath. "I told her my name was Alex. You promised."

"Alex, take a hike," Garrett ordered, gently steering him out of his work space. He turned back to Emily. "So, Ms. Taylor, what brings you down here? Checking up on your fan club out front?"

Emily felt her face flame. "I'm sorry about that. I would have thought they'd forgotten your column by now. I had no idea they were out there."

Garrett chuckled, then nodded. "Call me a fool, but I believe you, Ms. Taylor. It must be the lovely blush on your cheeks that convinced me."

Emily felt her cheeks redden to an even deeper shade. Lord, he was devastating when he turned on the charm. Her knees went weak at the same time her pulse decided to go wild and she found herself unable to think of a single thing to say. Thankfully, Garrett didn't share her lack of coherent speech.

"So, what can I do for you today, Ms. Taylor?"

"You—you can call me Emily," she suggested.

"That's easily done...Emily."

She wasn't prepared for the sound of her name on his lips. Emily alone was much more personal, more suggestive than Emily Taylor. As a child, she'd always hated her name, thought it too old-fashioned and a little prissy compared to Karen and Diane. But suddenly she decided it wasn't that bad, especially when spoken by Garrett McCabe.

"So," Garrett said. "You came here for...?" He waited for her to fill in the blank.

"Mushrooms," Emily blurted out. "There was a problem with my mushrooms."

"I'm so sorry," he said in mock sympathy. "Is there anything I can do to help?"

Emily drew a deep breath and tried to marshall her mental faculties. "In every issue we do a feature called 'Varieties,'" she explained. "Usually it's food and sometimes we tie it into vegetable gardening. This month we tried mushrooms, but the photo didn't turn out very well. Mushrooms have a habit of being a little dull. We've done tomatoes, winter squash, apples, peppers, anything that has a lot of variety and color."

He searched her gaze, an action that was both teasing and intimate. "What do these mushrooms have to do with me, Emily?"

"Nothing," Emily said. "Except, now we're going to use flowers instead. So I need you to take me to Descanso Gardens to see the camellias. Mr. Parker mentioned that you would be able to show me around Los Angeles. Don't you remember?"

"I remember quite well," he said dryly.

"So will you, Mr. McCabe?"

"Garrett," he said.

She swallowed convulsively. "Garrett," she repeated.

"Will I what?" he asked.

"Take me to see the camellias. It will give you an opportunity to see our magazine at work. I think you'll find the gardens very . . . interesting."

He nodded. "I'm sure I will. I just have to turn in my column and then I'll be all yours for the entire day."

All hers. For the entire day. Though the prospect might have sent other women into paroxysms of lust, Emily was not one of them. The prospect scared the wits out of her. She was unprepared to defend herself against Garrett McCabe's easy, inborn charm. In fact, she felt more comfortable when he was angry with her. She wondered if there was any way to restore the tension between them. First names certainly hadn't been a step in the right direction.

"Let's go, then," Garrett said. "I'll drop my copy on the way out."

"We have to leave through the side entrance," Emily explained. "I don't want the ladies out front to think I'm a scar."

Garrett laughed. "I'm sure they won't think you're a scar, or a scab either. They're big fans. But we should go out through the front door. You can sign a few autographs, thank them for their support, and tell them all to go home. And while you're at it, you can let them know I'm not as dumb as a post."

"No!" Emily cried in surge of panic.

Garrett's brow rose a few degrees. "All right, maybe I *am* as dumb as a post."

"Oh, no, that's not what I meant," she replied quickly, placing her hand on his forearm. "It's just that I couldn't go out there and talk to them. Strangers make me . . . uneasy. I never know what to say. *I* end up looking as dumb as a post."

Garrett studied her for a moment with a puzzled expression, then covered her fingers with his. "There's nothing to be frightened of," he said. "Most of them just want to tell you how much they like what you do. You just give them an autograph and send them on their way."

"I'm not comfortable with that," Emily said, nervously tugging her hand from beneath his. "At least, not yet." She paused. "Nora says that if we sell to Parker, he wants to put my picture on the cover of every issue."

"And you don't like the idea?"

Emily frowned. "Of course not. Would you?"

Garrett grabbed a folded newspaper from his desk and held it out to her. "They put my picture next to my column in the newspaper," he said.

"It doesn't look much like you," Emily said. "That must have made you happy."

"Happy?"

"People won't come up to you on the street and bother you."

"But that's the whole point. They're my fans, so I don't mind talking to them. It's part of the job. It sells papers. It boosts my career."

Emily sighed. "That's very brave," she murmured, genuine admiration in her voice. She didn't know Garrett McCabe well, but somehow she knew that his courage extended beyond a photo in the paper. There was an unshakable strength about him that seemed to extend to everything he saw, everyone he touched.

He smiled as he grabbed his jacket from the back of his desk chair and pulled it on. "Why don't you tell Parker you don't like the idea?"

"Nora says that I have to learn to be more comfortable with my public image. That if I'm not, Parker won't want to buy the magazine. Nora thinks that Parker Publishing will be the best thing that's ever happened to *At Home*. But I'm not so sure."

Garrett grabbed a sheaf of papers from his desk and directed her out of his office.

"So, you're not in favor of selling?" he asked as he dropped the papers in a basket at the end of the aisle.

"No, it's not that. It's just—I'm being silly. I guess I don't adapt to change very well. I sometimes like things to stay just the way they are."

"And sometimes a little change can be a good thing," Garrett said, placing his hand on the small of her back.

Her mind focussed on the feel of his fingers spread along the base of her spine. She sensed his energy seeping into her and she was tempted to stand perfectly still, unwilling to break the connection.

"That's what I'm afraid of," Emily murmured as she stepped into the elevator.

DAFFODILS. Before today, Garrett knew these flowers only as those yellow things that came up in the spring. But now he'd personally watched Emily Taylor examine every single variety of daffodil Descanso Gardens had planted. Whoever had named the flower had probably named it after spending the afternoon in a garden with a woman much like Emily—daffy.

If he ever had any hope of getting to know Emily Taylor better, those hopes were gone the moment they walked through the front gates. They began their afternoon with the camellia garden, but thankfully the over six hundred varieties were past their peak. If they hadn't been, he was certain they'd still be lost there, looking at variety number 217.

So they moved on to the outdoor orchids, which Emily found equally fascinating. After they looked at every one of those, she'd decided that the orchids were not a good choice, too exotic for her readership and not suitable in colder climates. After two hours of wandering, they were eliminated as a possible subject for her feature.

Somewhere along the line they had met up with an elderly botanist who was also visiting the garden. At first, Emily hung back, too shy to say much to him. But once they got past the introductions and onto the spring bulbs, they had become absorbed in deep discussion of the relative beauty of irises, tulips and daffodils. Emily was obviously impressed by the guy and his seemingly encyclopedic knowledge of mulch, bedding, bloom schedules and propagation. Garrett had been relegated to following the pair along the paths, bored out of his skull. All he knew was the next time he came upon a good-size pile of mulch, he'd have to fight the urge to toss Emily in, head first.

Geez, she could be exasperating. With all her attention focused on the flowers, she barely noticed he was there. He tried to recall what he found so attractive about her, but at that moment it eluded him. When she turned her energies in a certain direction, nothing stood in her way. He had to wonder what things might be like if she ever decided to turn that energy on him.

But maybe this was for the best. After all, he was obligated to report any conversations he had with Emily regarding the impending sale of *At Home*. If they didn't talk about it, he wouldn't have to pay another visit to Parker's office.

Her ears must have been burning at his frustrating musing. She turned around to look at him, sending him a dazzling smile. "Aren't they beautiful?" she called, with all the wonder of a child on Christmas morning in her voice.

Garrett froze in that instant, astonished by the sight before him. It was as if she belonged in this garden, amidst all this natural beauty, and he felt himself a heel for his earlier resentment. Her copper hair shimmered in the light, rumpled by the soft spring breeze, creating an angelic aura around her face. Her pale complexion was kissed pink by the California sun and sprinkled with tiny freckles. And her smile . . . her smile outshone the sheer radiance of every flower he'd seen. "Beautiful," he called, his voice catching in his throat.

She turned back to the botanist and continued her tour. Garrett's irritation seemed to evaporate into thin air as he watched her. She had an innate grace, gentle and unstudied. He dragged his gaze away and glanced down at the flower bed at his feet, silently controlling his overwhelming attraction to her. Strange how the flowers suddenly seemed more vivid.

By the time the botanist finally said his farewells, Garrett wasn't sure whether he trusted himself to be alone with her. Something had happened to him here among the flowers. It was as if he glimpsed a tiny corner of her world, a world filled with simple beauty and unfettered delight. A world he didn't understand and couldn't be a part of.

"I'd like to go look at the lilacs now," Emily said.

"Aren't you getting tired?" Garrett asked. "We've been at this for an awfully long time. We could go get something to eat."

"I don't want to miss anything," Emily replied. "Just the lilacs and then we can go."

As they hurried along the path, Emily read to him from the brochure, recounting the history of the gardens from the time the property was once part of the vast Spanish-owned Rancho San Rafael in the 1700s. The property also passed through the hands of an old newspaperman, E. Manchester Boddy, the owner and editor of the *Los Angeles Daily News*. Garrett had to admit that this gave him a greater appreciation of the place.

Emily suddenly stopped in midsentence and sniffed the air. "Can you smell them?" she asked.

He drew a breath through his nose and nodded. He smelled something but he hadn't a clue as to what it was.

"I have lilac bushes at home," she said. "Sometimes I walk into my garden and the spring air is thick with the smell. I fill vases full of them and for a few weeks in the spring, the house smells so lovely." She frowned. "I hope I don't miss the blooms this year."

They walked farther along the path and found the source of the scent. With a joyful giggle, she stepped into a huge bush and buried her face in the pale purple blossoms. Slowly, she turned around and faced him, pulling the flowers over her nose. "It's like heaven," she said, closing her eyes and inhaling deeply.

He wasn't sure what possessed him, whether it was the sight of her surrounded by flowers or the perfume that seemed to hang in the air like an aphrodisiac. Whatever it was, he couldn't resist and he stepped up to her and covered her mouth with his in a gentle kiss.

He felt her draw a sharp breath beneath his lips and he slowly opened his eyes to find her staring in wide-eyed terror from close range. Pulling back, he silently cursed his impulsive behavior, knowing he'd made a mistake. She wasn't like the women he knew, so familiar with the ways of desire, so schooled in the proper response. Emily Taylor was obviously untouched by the affectations of sexual experience.

But as he berated his actions, he watched in astonishment as a dazed smile touched her lips and color flooded her cheeks again. "Maybe we should move on to the roses," she murmured.

He smiled, then nodded his agreement. As they walked to the rose garden, he grabbed her hand and wove his fingers through hers. The move seemed perfectly natural and to his surprise, she didn't attempt to pull away. He liked the feel of her touch, so tentative and so delicate.

They strolled hand in hand along the paths that wove through the rose garden. Somewhere along the way, she lost her obsession with studying each individual flower. Instead, she explained what she knew of roses, which was an impressive amount. He listened as she spoke, not really hearing her words, but simply enjoying the musical lilt of her voice.

Somehow, he knew that he'd never look at a rose the same way again. Nor would he blithely order one or two dozen and send them to a woman he barely knew. Roses would always remind him of Emily Taylor, as would lilacs and daffodils.

"How do you know so much about roses?" he asked. "Better yet, how do you know so much about flowers and vegetables and pecan pies and cooking shrimp?"

She shrugged. "I don't know all that much."

"Yes, you do."

"I guess I just taught myself. Look, I love my work, but I don't pretend that it's all that important. One can't compare cooking shrimp to astrophysics, or making a pie crust to biochemistry."

"Who told you that?" Garrett asked.

"You did," she said with a rueful smile. "In your column. And most people would probably agree. I'm sure your readers did. And my ex-husband certainly shared that viewpoint."

She stopped as if she had suddenly revealed too much. Her voice became remote, uncertain, and he saw a tiny glimmer of hurt in her eyes. Her pain went right to his heart as he realized that he had been the cause.

"Emily, I'm sorry if I said anything in my column that hurt you. It wasn't meant to be a personal attack."

"I know," she said softly. "I guess I just have to learn to be a little tougher, more immune to things like that."

"I think you're a pretty tough lady," Garrett said. "Look at what you've done with your books and your magazine. You don't get to where you are in publishing without grit and determination."

"I'm a wimp," Emily admitted. "I've never been an assertive person. I did the books because I had no other choice. I didn't know how to do anything else."

"You could give yourself a little more credit, Emily. You're a very talented lady."

She looked up at him. "Do you really think so?"

Garrett nodded. "Really." He stared at her for a long moment, trying to decide whether to kiss her again.

"Maybe we should go," she murmured.

"If that's what you want," Garrett said, not bothering to hide the disappointment in his voice.

The drive back to the Malibu beach house was filled with impersonal chitchat about their day at the gardens. He could tell that Emily was flustered by her earlier candidness and for the first time, he felt a nagging curiosity toward the man that had once been her husband.

What had brought about their divorce? She certainly couldn't have been the cause. She would have been the perfect wife, a woman any man would be proud to call his own. The fault must have fallen with her husband. He was tempted to probe further, but Emily didn't seem anxious to reveal any more about her marriage.

"Where would you like to go tomorrow?" he asked when the silence between them had dragged on too long.

"What?" she said, turning away from the window to look at him.

"Tomorrow," he repeated. "You might enjoy the Farmers' Market. We could go in the afternoon and have an early dinner. There are all sorts of food stalls there. If I were you, I wouldn't bother with breakfast and lunch. We'll eat our way around the market."

"I—I don't know," she said. "I have to take care of the 'Varieties' feature. There are arrangements to be made, people to call. I've got to explain everything to the photographer. I'm not sure how long it will take. Maybe all day."

Garrett refused to take her excuse as a no. "Why don't I pick you up at the beach house around two?" he suggested. "Take my word as your tour guide—you'll enjoy this. I guarantee it."

She hesitated for a moment, then forced a smile. "I—I'll call you tomorrow and let you know if it doesn't work into my schedule."

Little more was said between them until Garrett pulled into the driveway of the beach house. This time, Emily didn't wait for him to hop out and open her door. And she didn't invite him inside for coffee and pie. Instead, she pushed the door open herself, jumped out, gave him a quick goodbye, before she hurried up the sidewalk and into the house.

Garrett sat in the car for a full ten minutes before he backed out of the driveway. For someone who wore her heart on her sleeve, Emily Taylor certainly had her mysterious side. And Garrett McCabe was more determined than ever to find out more about the woman he'd kissed among the flowers.

5

"YOU'RE MAKING croissants. It must be serious."

Emily stared through the window of the oven door, trying to gauge whether her croissants had reached the perfect shade of golden brown. She checked the timer once more before she looked back over her shoulder at Nora. Her friend stood in the middle of the kitchen, dressed in her tattered chenille bathrobe and fuzzy slippers, her signature topknot askew. "Why do you always try to attach some hidden motive to my baking?" she asked. "Maybe I just wanted fresh croissants for breakfast."

Nora sat down on a stool and rubbed her sleepy eyes. "Fresh-baked croissants for breakfast at 8:00 means you started baking around 2:00 in the morning. Which means you couldn't sleep. Which means you've got something serious on your mind." She yawned and stretched her arms above her head. "Which means you better tell me what it is because you know I'll pry it out of you sooner or later."

Emily poured a cup of coffee and pushed it across the breakfast bar to Nora. Why did she even try to keep her problems to herself? Her baking habits always gave her away. Maybe she should consider taking up another activity when under stress—like pacing, or chewing her fingernails, or even weeping uncontrollably. Maybe then she'd be able to fool Nora.

But the truth be told, she *was* preoccupied. And the source of her sleeplessness had been Garrett Mc-Cabe...and the kiss they had shared. She had relived the moment over and over as she tried to fall asleep, each time attempting to rationalize the overwhelming desire she had felt when his lips touched hers. Maybe it was that Garrett McCabe was an unusually talented kisser . . . or that she'd been too long without romance in her life . . . or even worse, that she harbored some secret fantasy about the man.

All she knew was that she'd never felt that way with Eric, so breathless and dizzy and filled with a strange anticipation. Eric had regarded affection as a husband's duty, with overt demonstrations reserved for birthdays and anniversaries. And it had been her wifely obligation to respond appropriately. But she was nearly certain these unfamiliar yearnings she had for Garrett McCabe had nothing to do with obligation. She had enjoyed his kiss, and had wanted more.

But what? She fought back a rush of embarrassment and silently chastised herself. She couldn't possibly want *that!* After all, she had never really enjoyed *that*. Besides, nice girls *did not* lust after men they barely knew. In fact, according to her mother, nice girls didn't lust at all. It only got them in trouble.

But wasn't it natural to lust? Though she'd been brought up in a rather repressed atmosphere, she'd seen enough in magazines and on television to know that women could now be open about their sexual needs. Though she'd completely missed the sexual revolution, sheltered from all the sweeping change by her very proper and unliberated mother, that didn't mean she couldn't enjoy the benefits now.

Still, she wasn't sure what she was feeling could be classified as lust. Maybe she was beginning to have feelings for Garrett. After her divorce, she'd vowed that she'd never let herself fall in love again, never give a man such power and control over her. And to that end, she'd managed to put plenty of distance between herself and the opposite sex—until now. Whatever it was, love or lust, she couldn't seem to stop herself. And she wasn't sure she wanted to.

"You were already in bed when I got home last night," Nora commented, watching her over the rim of her coffee cup. "I didn't get a chance to ask how your day with Garrett McCabe went."

Emily swallowed hard. "Fine. The gardens were beautiful. The camellias were past their prime, but the layout of the rose garden was exquisite. And the spring bulbs were fantastic. I've decided we'll do 'Varieties' on bulbs. We'll show the bulb and a fresh cut flower next to it. I think it would be the best if we—"

"I don't give a fig about the flowers, Em," Nora said. "What happened with you and Garrett?"

Emily tried to compose herself and concentrate on a plausible story. "Well, first we walked through the camellias, and then we took a look at the outdoor orchids. I met a botanist who was visiting the garden. After that we—"

"Em, please," Nora said in frustration. "Don't play dumb. You know exactly what I'm talking about, now cut to the chase."

She hadn't deliberately been playing dumb, but if Nora was determined to butt into her business, again, so be it! "All right!" Emily snapped. "He—he kissed me. And I kissed him back. Are you satisfied now?"

Nora smiled then took a long sip from her coffee cup. She slowly placed it back in the saucer. "Quite. And what about you?"

Emily crossed her arms beneath her breasts and shifted from foot to foot. "What do you mean, what about me?"

"Was it satisfying for you?"

Yes! her mind screamed. *No!* her conscience countered. "How should I know?" she replied defensively. "I suppose his kiss was quite nice as kisses go. Not that I have a whole lot to compare it to. I've only ever been kissed by one other man in my life and that was Eric." She paused again. "And Johnny Kelly in the second grade, but that doesn't count because it was on the cheek."

"So how was it?"

"As I remember, it was horribly embarrassing. It happened at recess and all the kids in the class were watching and I—"

Nora shot her an impatient glare. "Not Johnny Kelly, Em. Garrett McCabe. Let's try to stick to the subject here."

Emily drew a deep breath and fixed the memory in her mind. "It was . . . horribly embarrassing . . . and incredibly wonderful at the same time. My knees started shaking and I felt like I couldn't breathe and my mind was whirling around faster than the frappé speed on my blender."

"That's good!" Nora said.

"And then I remembered what a failure I am when it comes to men and I told him we'd better move along to the roses."

"That's not so good," Nora said. "Not exactly what I would have done if Garrett McCabe had kissed *me*. I would have pulled him into the bushes and had my way with him right then and there." She sighed longingly. "Then again, he didn't kiss me, he kissed you."

"That is *exactly* the point. You would have known what to do, I didn't. I met Eric when I was sixteen. I married him when I was eighteen. And I can't remember falling in love. It's all like a dim childhood memory."

"If I were you, I'd wish for complete amnesia when it comes to Eric."

Emily opened the oven door and pulled out the sheet of perfectly baked croissants. "I didn't know how to behave or what to say. I didn't know what order things came in.

Should I have let him kiss me so soon? We hadn't even held hands yet. Holding hands should come before kissing. And then there was the tongue thing. I know I made a huge mistake there."

"Why don't you explain the tongue thing to me and let me judge," Nora said.

Emily felt a blush creep up her cheeks. "You know! French kissing. I know I'm not supposed to do that on the first date. But this wasn't really a date . . . which, I guess, makes it worse, doesn't it? I just got carried away and now he's going to think I'm easy . . . which couldn't be further from the truth. I'm about as *uneasy* as they come."

Nora snatched a croissant from the baking sheet and tossed it back and forth between her hands until it cooled. "Em, let me tell you something and I want you to listen very carefully. You're an adult now. You have been for quite some time. And as an adult, you get to make up your own rules as you go along. If you want to kiss Garrett McCabe standing on your head in the middle of Wilshire Boulevard during rush hour—with tongue—you can do it."

"See there," Emily said, placing her palms on her burning cheeks. "I didn't even know the rule about no rules for adults. I can make a perfect soufflé, I can grow aphid-free roses, I can whip up a pair of pinch-pleated drapes in one afternoon. But I have no idea how to act around a man. As I see it, I have only one choice."

"And what would that be?"

"I have to stay well out of the range of Garrett McCabe's lips from now on," she replied.

Nora shook her head. "Why? If I were you, I'd take this opportunity to expand your knowledge. Think of it as self-improvement."

"Well, I'm not you and I'm not interested in self-improvement."

"You didn't sew a perfect pair of pinch-pleats the first time out of the block, did you?"

"No, it took lots of practice to get those pleats to hang exactly right. But kissing Garrett McCabe is different. I never got wobbly knees making drapes. And I always knew exactly where I was and what I was doing. And, unlike Garrett McCabe, my sewing machine only makes a move when I press the foot pedal."

Nora pulled the warm croissant apart with her fingers and popped a piece into her mouth. "Well, I think a little kissing might do you some good."

"I'm not good at relationships with men, Nora. My marriage proved that."

"You're basing this theory on one relationship with a selfish jerk, a relationship that was over years ago. Besides, just because you kiss Garrett McCabe a few times does not mean you have to marry him. It doesn't even mean that you have a relationship. After the sale goes through, you can go back home and continue your life, as if nothing happened, all the better for the experience."

"I couldn't do that," Emily said. "It just wouldn't be right."

"Why not? Be assertive. Take what you want. And that includes Garrett McCabe—and his lips." Nora stuffed the remainder of her croissant in her mouth, then took a gulp of her coffee. "So, when are you going to see him again?"

"He wants to take me to the Farmers' Market later this afternoon. He's picking me up at 2:00...unless I call him and tell him not to." Emily stared at the phone at the end of the counter. "I'd better call him."

Nora glanced up at the kitchen clock. "Don't. Just get some sleep. Considering your current state of mind, you're definitely going to want to have all your wits about you. And you are looking a little ragged around the edges."

Emily bent to examine her reflection in the oven door. "But I can't spend the afternoon with him. I've got to take care of the 'Varieties' feature. I made a list of all the bulbs we want to cover. We'll need to contact the gardens and see if we can get cut flowers and bulbs."

"Give me your list. You just crawl back into bed and I'll take care of everything."

Emily shook her head reluctantly. "I'm not going to get involved with Garrett McCabe. That would be a bigger mistake than marrying Eric. What's the point? We're going to be leaving as soon as we wrap up our business here."

"Not necessarily," Nora said with a tight smile. "Parker wants us to consider moving our offices out here."

"To California?" Emily gasped. "Absolutely not! I'm not moving out here."

"And why not?" Nora asked.

"There are no seasons here, for one. *At Home* revolves around the seasons. Our winter issues will look exactly like our summer issues. And I'd get really tired of sunshine day in and day out. I like the rain and the snow."

"And the ice and the bitter cold. Em, we can always go back east for our seasonal features," Nora explained. "And the bad weather, if you prefer."

"But, I'd have to leave my house and my favorite market and the best produce man in Rhode Island. And what about my favorite garden center. And my gardens, for that matter. It's taken me years to get my perennials established. Oh, and my roses. I could never be happy here without my roses."

"Well, just think about it," Nora said. "It's up to us whether we move the editorial offices or not."

"*If* we decide to sell," Emily said, "we'll discuss it then. But I haven't made my decision yet."

Nora's brow furrowed in concern. "Why are you hesitating, Em? Can't you see that Parker Publishing would be the best thing for us? I've looked at all the figures, I've covered every detail with Richard Parker and his people and you've read all the reports. What's holding you back?"

She shrugged. "I just don't like the fact that we'll be giving up our controlling interest. Richard Parker is going to run the magazine and we'll just collect a paycheck. It doesn't seem right. After all, the magazine has my name on it. It's ours, yours and mine."

"Em, we'll still have absolute control over the creative. All the contracts assure us of that. Besides, *At Home* is just too big for us to take the risks anymore. Let Richard Parker take the financial risks. And won't it be nice to get paid every month? If you remember, there was a stretch a few years back, when we switched to the oversize format, when we didn't take home a cent from *At Home*."

"I know, I know. But something tells me we shouldn't give up control. Call it gut instinct or feminine intuition, I'm not sure what it is."

"I think you're projecting," Nora said.

"Now I'm projecting? I thought I was transferring," Emily said with a frown.

"You're doing both. You're projecting your insecurities and doubts about Garrett McCabe onto the deal with Parker Publishing. It's Garrett McCabe you're not so sure about."

On this subject, Nora was right. Emily understood Garrett McCabe even less than she understood their deal with Parker, and that was precious little. "Maybe so," Emily admitted. "After all, what do I know about business? You're the whiz in that area."

Nora slipped off the chair and circled the breakfast bar, then put her arm around Emily. "We're partners, Em, and we won't sign this deal until you feel completely comfortable with it. There are lots of publishers out there who would love to buy our magazine. If you don't like Parker, we'll find someone else."

"But Parker is the best, right?" Emily smiled hesitantly. "It's not that I don't trust you, Nora. But since we've come to California, I've been so—confused. Back home, my life was so orderly, so predictable. Things are so different here."

"You're just tired. Go back to bed and get some rest. I'll call the *Post* and tell Garrett McCabe that you're busy this afternoon."

"Thanks," Emily said with a rush of relief. She glanced around at the mess in the kitchen. Suddenly, she was too exhausted to even think about cleaning up. All she wanted to do was crawl under the covers and sleep for the next week or two. Things were changing too quickly for her and she couldn't keep up. If only she could forget about Garrett McCabe and the strange feelings he aroused in her. If she was back home, she'd lose herself in her garden, begin a new decorating project and work on her French cooking. And then everything would feel safe and secure.

But until the deal was signed or rejected, Emily was stuck in California. And somehow she sensed that as long as Garrett McCabe was in her life, she'd never really feel safe.

SHE SLEPT FITFULLY, tossing and turning and drifting between sleep and wakefulness. She dreamt that she was in one of Nora's self-improvement classes, an assertiveness training class, with a teacher who wore a dress, but looked suspiciously like General George Patton.

The classroom was huge and filled with people. She sat near the back, hoping that no one would call on her. But then, the teacher pointed in her direction, and she found herself walking up to the front of the class. She tried to stop, but it was as if her legs had a will of their own. Suddenly, a huge door appeared in the middle of the aisle. She rang the bell, but no one answered. She knocked, but the door remained closed. Somehow, she sensed that this was an important lesson and that she was expected to find her way through the door. Ringing and knocking and ringing and knocking...

Emily forced her eyes open and the classroom disappeared. But the ringing and knocking continued. The afternoon light filtered through the curtains and she blinked, then glanced over at the bedside clock. 2:00 p.m. What was it that was supposed to happen at 2:00? Slowly, her mind cleared. Oh, Lord. Could Garrett McCabe be at her door?

Emily threw the covers back and jumped out of bed, then scrambled to find her bathrobe. She tugged the soft pink flannel robe over her white nightgown and hurried to the door. A quick check through the peephole proved her suspicions accurate. She delicately cursed Nora Griswold and her meddling ways. Now that she knew Garrett McCabe was on the other side of the door, she wasn't sure what to do. She couldn't let him in, not while she was still in her nightgown. It wouldn't be proper.

The doorbell rang again, followed by a rapid knocking. She could open the door and tell him to go away. Or she could make him stand outside while she got ready. Refusing to answer the door seemed to be her best option, though that bordered on blatant rudeness. He would think she forgot about their plans and Emily Taylor never missed an appointment. She reached out to turn the dead bolt then slowly opened the door a crack. His face appeared in the sliver of sunlight.

"Emily? Is everything all right?" he asked. "When you didn't answer the door, I thought—"

"I—I'm not ready," she interrupted, peering at him from her place behind the door.

Garrett glanced at his watch. "I'm not early, am I? We did say 2:00."

"No . . . no, you're right on time. It's just that Nora was supposed to call you and tell you that I was . . . busy."

"You don't look busy to me," Garrett said.

Mortified by being caught in a lie, Emily struggled to maintain her composure. "It will only take me a few minutes to get ready. I'll be right out." She slammed the door and shot the lock home, then started across the room. But the sound of another knock at the door stopped her in her tracks. Hesitantly, she returned to the door and opened it again.

Garrett gave her a little wave. "Aren't you going to ask me in?"

"I—I'm not dressed," Emily said.

His brow raised a few degrees and he craned his neck to see inside.

"I mean, I'm dressed, but I'm not wearing clothes." She laughed nervously. "I mean, I *am* wearing clothes. Just my nightgown. And my robe. I was taking a nap and I overslept."

"We're both adults here, Ms. Taylor. I think I'm mature enough to handle the sight of you in your bathrobe. Now, why don't you let me in so I can wait inside."

Every instinct told her to close the door and lock it. The first time Eric had seen her in her nightgown was on their wedding night and she remembered very vividly where *that* had led. But, like Nora had said earlier, adults got to make up their own rules. And she and Garrett McCabe were adults. If she wanted to let him in the house, she certainly could. She didn't want him to think she was a complete prude! And who was she to assume that the sight of Emily

Taylor in a nightgown would call forth Garrett McCabe's animal instincts?

Screwing up her courage, she slowly opened the door, clutching at the neckline of her robe. Garrett stepped inside. Chagrined, she watched as his gaze drifted from her head to her toes. A smile quirked the corners of his mouth.

"I'd better get dressed, now," she murmured.

"That would probably be a good idea," Garrett said. "An outfit like that is guaranteed to test any man's self-control. I find all that pink flannel very...provocative."

Her eyes widened and she swallowed convulsively, before she realized he was teasing her. Her cheeks warmed in embarrassment. Lord, he must think she was such a nitwit. "I'll be right back," she said. "Why don't you...wait here?"

Emily raced to the bedroom and slammed the door behind her. She had to be out of her mind. How in the world would she be able to spend the rest of the afternoon with Garrett McCabe? Her heart was already in her throat and somewhere between the front door and her bedroom, her legs had gone boneless. She felt as if all her common sense had just disappeared. Assertiveness was a noble concept, but much easier said than done.

On the other hand, he seemed to be quite calm. He obviously didn't have any immoral intentions or he would have displayed them when he found her in her nightgown. But a man like Garrett McCabe probably appreciated an experienced woman, a woman well versed in the ways of the flesh. And the only flesh Emily felt entirely familiar with was raw poultry.

"I can handle an afternoon with Garrett McCabe," she chanted to herself. "I am an adult. I am not a nitwit. I can do this. I can." She paused. "Just as long as he doesn't kiss me."

Throwing the closet door open, Emily frantically searched for something appropriate to wear. But nothing in her wardrobe of conservative dresses appealed to her at that moment. She longed for a sophisticated dress or stylish jacket. Or even a casual blouse. But as she scanned the contents of the closet over and over again, she realized how fixated she was on practical, inconspicuous dresses—all made from some type of daintily flowered fabric. After ten minutes of concentrated effort, she grabbed a loose fitting calico jumper and tossed it on the bed.

But rather than retrieve the simple cotton blouse with the Peter Pan collar she usually wore under it, she dug a chemise out of her underwear drawer and pulled it over her head. Then she tugged the jumper on and opened the top three buttons, revealing the tiny flowers at the neckline of the chemise.

She felt positively wicked not wearing a bra, but the thin straps of the jumper and chemise eliminated that choice. Her arms and chest were bare so she rummaged through her drawer until she found a serviceable sweater to take along in case the weather turned cool. The canvas tennies and ankle socks she wore for her morning walk completed her new look.

Emily stared into the full-length mirror on the back of the bedroom door and sighed. She was showing a lot more skin than she had in her nightgown and robe, but she didn't feel nearly as naked. In fact, she felt a little . . . sexy. After running her fingers through her rumpled hair, she reached for her brush, but stopped before she tugged it through her tangled curls. She'd leave her hair as it was.

Emily drew a deep breath and consciously tried to calm her nerves. She would show Garrett McCabe she wasn't some silly little housewife with butter for brains. After all, she looked different now, relaxed, in a California kind of way. Too bad her new look didn't bother to convey her relaxation to the knot in her stomach.

She found Garrett waiting for her where she'd left him, at the door. "Why didn't you come in and sit down?" she asked.

"You told me to wait here," Garrett replied with an easy grin.

He was teasing her again. She smiled hesitantly and tried to suppress the blush that threatened. When Garrett McCabe turned on the charm, he was a hard man to resist. But resist him she would.

"You look very nice," he said, his gaze raking her figure from top to bottom.

"I—I just pulled any old thing out of the closet," Emily said. Never mind that it had taken her ten minutes of frantic searching to do it. Or that she wasn't really sure she didn't look like a fashion disaster. She'd never paid much attention to her wardrobe before, but then again, she'd never been trying to impress a man, either.

He grabbed her hand and laced his fingers through hers. "Then if you're ready, let's go."

She glanced down at their intertwined hands, then back up at his face. It took her a moment to remember to breathe. "I guess I am," she murmured as she tugged her hand from his and opened the door. "As ready as I'll ever be."

They drove along the coast highway with the top down, the warm spring wind buffeting through the convertible. The sky above them was a brilliant blue and Emily could smell the ocean in the air. If someone would have told her a few months ago that she would one day be speeding down a California highway in a sports car with a handsome man at the wheel, she would have written the person off as insane.

She turned her face up to the sun and closed her eyes, trying to calm her nerves. I am not attracted to Garrett McCabe, she chanted inwardly. Garrett McCabe is not the right man for me. I don't need a man in my life to be happy.

The touch of his hand on her cheek startled her and she opened her eyes and turned to him. As they waited at a red light, he gently brushed a strand of her hair from her face. Their gazes locked for a long moment and her heart stopped in her chest. She couldn't move, couldn't speak. Every cell in her brain was focused on the warmth of his fingers, the tingling of her skin. Then, as quickly as his touch had come, it was gone and he turned his attention back to the road.

Emily's mind whirled. So much for affirmations. One touch and all her resolve disappeared. But what did it all mean? Was it a gesture of affection, or was he simply trying to push the hair out of her eyes? She wished she had brought Nora along to answer these questions, because when it came to matters like this, she herself didn't have a clue.

"Are you hungry?" Garrett asked.

"Not really," Emily said. Right now, she wasn't sure she could even swallow much less chew. Then she suddenly remembered where they were going and why. "I mean, yes, I'm famished. I haven't eaten all day."

Garrett chuckled, shaking his head. "Do you always say what you think other people want to hear?"

"No," Emily said. "Well, maybe. Sometimes."

Garrett flipped on the turn signal, then pulled into a space in the Farmers' Market lot. He shut off the ignition and began to raise the convertible top of the car. "You are terminally polite, aren't you?"

Emily blinked in surprise. "What's wrong with that? I'm just trying to be nice."

"You are nice," Garrett said, pushing his door open. "But that shouldn't stop you from being honest. Now, are you, or are you not, hungry? Go ahead," he said solemnly. "I can handle the truth."

She smiled as Garrett helped her out of the car. "All right, I'm not hungry now. But I will be soon."

The Farmers' Market took up a huge area in the Wilshire District on Third and Fairfax. Emily had read that in the early thirties, the market stood on the edge of the city, conveniently located for the farmers who worked the surrounding land and hauled their produce to the cooperative. But now, Los Angeles and its suburbs sprawled for miles in any direction, turning the market into a tiny island from the past.

Emily gazed up at the clock tower and drew a deep breath. An exotic blend of smells touched her nose, beckoning her inside the open-air market. Produce and meat, cheese and bakery goods, even flowers, were all sold fresh from stands. Restaurants offered cuisines from all corners of the world and gift shops were scattered throughout the market, filled with unusual imports and handmade crafts.

A surge of excitement rushed through Emily. Garrett had sensed that she'd like this place and he was right. Maybe he *was* beginning to understand her.

"This is wonderful," Emily said.

"Where would you like to start?" Garrett asked.

She wanted to start by throwing her arms around his neck and kissing him the way he'd kissed her among the lilacs. But no matter how forceful she tried to be, she couldn't picture herself acting on such an impulse again. She tried to summon her resolve but the sight of fresh seafood distracted her and she forgot the notion altogether.

The market was bustling with people, both tourists and locals. Though Emily usually didn't like large crowds, she felt comfortable with Garrett at her side, and soon she was picking over the produce as if she'd shopped there her entire life.

Every now and then, they'd stop at a food stand and share a bit of international cuisine before moving on. The tastes, the smells, the noise, all combined to make the market hum with a contagious energy, distracting her at every turn. The afternoon seemed to fly by and Emily couldn't remember the last time she'd enjoyed herself so much.

She decided it was time to quit when she couldn't stuff another bag into Garrett's arms. Though he was trying to act as if he enjoyed trailing her from stand to stand, he suddenly looked like a man who'd just been told he needed major dental work. It wasn't hard to see that Garrett was not a happy shopper. She chided herself for not noticing sooner. "Maybe it's time to go home," Emily suggested.

"Already?" Garrett asked, dropping his armload of bags on a bench. "But we've only been here for three hours." One of the bags split open and a yellow pepper thumped to his feet. He gave it a swift kick, sending it skittering down an aisle. "I was sort of hoping I'd get the chance to break the world record for bench pressing produce."

He was definitely perturbed. It didn't take a genius to figure that one out. "We could have left earlier," Emily said softly, a hint of defensiveness creeping into her voice. "Why didn't you say something?"

"And miss all the excitement? I've never seen anyone get so crazy over fresh vegetables. I figured if I tried to tear you away, you'd attack me with an one of those vicious-looking eggplants you bought."

"You make it sound like I'm obsessed."

"You said it, not me," he countered.

"Fresh produce is a very important part of a nutritious diet," she replied. "The fresher, the better. It's always a challenge to find the best."

"And is that the party line on produce? If it is, it's not very convincing. I'll take a taco any day."

Emily braced her hands on her hips. "Why are you angry? And why are you blaming me? You're the one who told me we could go wherever *I* wanted."

"I didn't think you'd want to hit every one of the one hundred and fifty stands. I thought we'd spend a nice afternoon together, talking and strolling and eating. I didn't expect to embark on a frenzied quest for the perfect plum tomato. This would make a great column. 'My Day at the Farmers' Market' by Garrett McCabe."

"I wouldn't expect you to understand," she murmured. She grabbed a bag in each hand and headed toward the car.

"And what is that supposed to mean?" Garrett called, scrambling to collect the rest of her purchases. He fumbled with the bags, trying hard to keep them all in his arms while grabbing another.

She turned and watched him as he followed her. "It means that I was naive to believe that you'd ever comprehend what it is I do, or what truly interests me," Emily said. "And be careful, there are peaches in that bag!"

"Oh, I comprehend it all right," Garrett replied. "But that doesn't mean I have to enjoy it. I just don't like taking a back seat to a bunch of fruits and vegetables."

"Is that why you're angry?" she asked.

"I'm angry because I don't necessarily enjoy shopping," he said, continuing on past her. Emily hurried to catch up, studying him covertly. "Not many men do, yet we always seem to get sucked into it. You've seen them, haven't you? Those poor saps with the zombie stares, trailing around after their shop-happy wives from one mall to another. There's one now," he said, cocking his head to the left. "And there's another. And another. Sort of like the Stepford husbands. Pretty scary, don't you think?"

"Just what are you trying to say?" Emily asked.

Garrett shoved his key into the car door, yanked it open and began to toss the bags in the back seat. With that done, he worked on lowering the convertible's top. "I'm saying we just wasted an entire afternoon doing something that could have been accomplished within ten minutes at a minimart."

Emily studied him with a frown. This was not about her shopping habits, this was about him! Suddenly it all became clear. "You're jealous, aren't you?"

Garrett gasped. "Where would you get a ridiculous idea like that?" He slid into the driver's seat and turned the ignition, then watched as the top folded back.

Emily smiled smugly. "You are. You're jealous of a bunch of vegetables. You're mad because I wasn't paying enough attention to you."

"What?" Garrett cried. "I brought you here because Richard Parker ordered me to show you around Los Angeles and that's it."

"I thought you said you brought me here so we could spend a nice afternoon together."

"If that was my original intent, then I was seriously deluded. Now get in the car."

Emily climbed into the passenger seat, then twisted around to rearrange the bags in the back of the Mustang. "Produce should be carefully handled," she said. "Throwing it around will ruin it."

"I'll remember that little tip the next time I shop for produce," Garrett said. "Which, judging from the fun I had today, should be sometime in the twenty-third century."

Emily settled back into the seat for the long, and probably silent, ride home. What had started out as a promising afternoon, had turned into a virtual disaster, but she wasn't quite sure what had caused it. Garrett was the one who wanted to show her the Farmers' Market. She hadn't asked him to bring her here. Yet, he seemed to be angry because she'd truly enjoyed herself.

Who wouldn't enjoy an afternoon at a market like that? Emily crossed her arms in front of her and pouted. Garrett McCabe, for one. And, in all honesty, probably a few other men on the planet. So, maybe she *had* gone a little overboard. But if he didn't bring her to the market to shop, why, then? A reason came to mind, but she wrote it off as too outlandish.

Could he really have brought her to the market to enjoy her company for the afternoon? And had she completely missed his intent and paid more attention to the produce than to him? Emily found it hard to believe that a man like Garrett McCabe would feel resentful of something as silly as veggies. But then, she had to admit, she didn't know much about the inner workings of the male ego.

But she did know enough to realize that Garrett had an uncanny talent for turning the blame on her. After all, he'd blamed her for the problems caused by *his* column. And now, he was mad because *he* chose to bring her to the Farmers' Market and *she* had enjoyed it. Well, she was getting a little tired of taking all the blame. She wasn't about to apologize!

Emily opened the bag on her lap and slowly picked through the contents, removing a fresh crab and placing it on the dashboard of his car while she examined another. She felt Garrett's gaze on her, but she refused to acknowledge it, putting the crabs back in the bag in her own sweet time. He was just like Eric, so self-absorbed and egotistical and bent on having his own way.

When they finally reached the beach house, she was out of the car before he had a chance to put it in park. She grabbed the bags of produce from the back seat, trying to pile them all in her arms.

"I'll help you with those," Garrett said.

"Don't bother," Emily said. "Considering your aversion to vegetable shopping, I wouldn't want to make you haul them inside as well." She dropped a bag and a half dozen tomatoes rolled across the back seat.

"Dammit, Emily, I said I'd help you. Now put those bags down."

He came around to her side of the car and snatched a bag from her hands. She tried to take it back, but he'd have none of it and he turned and started for the house. In a fit of frustration, Emily reached into the back seat and grabbed a tomato, whipping it in his direction.

She never meant to hit him. In fact, in her entire life she couldn't remember ever hitting anything she aimed for. But the tomato contacted his left shoulder with a solid *thwack* and splattered over the fabric of his jacket and the side of his neck. Well, at least she knew the tomatoes were ripe.

He stopped in his tracks and reached up to wipe a blob of seeds and pulp from below his ear. Then he turned around to face her. Slowly, he approached, a fierce expression on his handsome face. She hurried to grab another tomato and pulled her arm back to throw it.

But he caught her wrist in his hand, holding it so tightly she was forced to drop her weapon. They stared at each other for a long moment, the tension humming between them like a live wire, his hand branding her skin with its heat. And then the unthinkable happened.

In one wild, impetuous moment, she threw her arms around his neck and pulled his mouth down to hers. The kiss was intense, filled with years of repressed sexual desire. Slowly, his mouth opened and she teased at his lips with her tongue, as if to prove something to herself, and maybe to him. If Garrett thought he could push her around, she'd show him exactly how wrong he was.

But then she heard a moan rumbling deep in his chest and the haze that had settled over them suddenly cleared. What was she doing? She'd never initiated a sexual encounter in her life! This wasn't assertiveness or courage, this was sheer lunacy. Common sense set in and she quickly jerked away.

She could see the passion in his eyes, could hear his quickened breathing. Oh, Lord, what had she done? With a tiny cry of dismay, Emily placed her fingers over her tingling lips. Then, gathering her wits, she raced past Garrett into the house. She didn't feel safe until she'd reached her bedroom and locked the door behind her. For good measure, she hurried into the bathroom and locked that door behind her as well.

But no matter how many doors stood between them, there was no way to erase her embarrassment. And no way to stem the flood of desire that raced through her body. She'd kissed Garrett McCabe and she had actually enjoyed it!

She was definitely in trouble now.

6

"THE TEAM BUS LEAVES at dawn." The voice on the other end of the phone line was barely audible.

Garrett pulled the phone away from his ear and knocked it on his desk, then listened again. "What?" he asked.

"The team bus leaves at dawn," Alvin whispered. "Now give me the counter code."

"Alvin—I mean Alex—it's me. Garrett McCabe. You're the one who dialed my number. What do you have for me?"

"Come on, Mr. McCabe. How do I know it's really you unless you give me the code? You remember," he prompted. "The cheerleaders will be . . ."

"Armstrong, stand up." Garrett watched over the top of his cubicle as Alvin's head popped up from the sports department at the far end of the newsroom, the phone pressed to his ear. He waved and Alvin hesitantly waved back. "See there. It's me. Now, tell me what you have."

"I have the information you asked for—about—you know who. I think we should meet to discuss it."

"Then come over here and we'll talk," Garrett said.

"I don't think we should talk in the newsroom," Alvin said. "Let's rendezvous at the—you know where. Midnight. Be there. I'll be wearing a blue jacket and a Dodgers cap."

"I'm not waiting until midnight. Make it seven," Garrett said. "And Armstrong?"

"Yes, Mr. McCabe?"

"The cheerleaders will be wearing very short skirts." He dropped his phone back into the cradle. This secret agent stuff was guaranteed to drive him crazy in short order. But if it kept Alvin happy, he'd have to go along. Without Alvin and his mail room buddy, he had no way to learn what was going on in Richard Parker's devious mind.

Not that he should care. After his recent run-in with Emily Taylor and her laser-guided vegetables, he wasn't sure he even wanted to be her self-appointed protector. With an aim like hers, she could protect herself. Garrett stifled a laugh. He had to admit, her sudden attack of assertiveness had surprised the hell out of him. And that kiss had really knocked him for a loop.

Even after a few days, he still remembered the feel of her mouth pressed firmly, frantically, to his, her soft lips parting slightly, giving him a tantalizing taste of the possibilities that stood between them. What had it taken for her to drop her defenses and overcome her insecurities? To gather her courage and throw herself into his arms? Whatever it was—frustration, anger, desire—it really didn't matter.

It didn't change the fact that he and Emily lived on different planets, and always would. The trip to the Farmers' Market only proved that. By the end of the day, any notion he had of starting a relationship with her had been wiped completely from his mind.

He could just imagine the two them—together. He'd be ready for the asylum before they celebrated their one month anniversary. His mind drifted in other directions. Not that there wouldn't be a few advantages to starting a relationship with her. Exploring the real woman beneath that reserved facade could keep a man busy for a good long time. Emily certainly wasn't hard to look at. In fact, he found endless interest in watching her. And the meals wouldn't be bad.

But she had certain expectations when it came to a relationship and Garrett would never be able to live up to them. She deserved nothing less than a happily-ever-after and he wasn't the one to give it to her. He wasn't willing to give up his free and easy life, and his career, for the responsibilities of a lifelong commitment.

So why was he considering a course that might result in losing his job over her? If Richard Parker even suspected Garrett was poking into his business dealings, Garrett would be out on the street without another column inch to his name. But then, Garrett McCabe rarely paid attention to what was good for him.

He'd met with Parker that morning and had given him information that he knew was useless. Though Parker was disappointed, Garrett promised to try harder to gain Emily's confidence and that seemed to satisfy him. The man was dangerous, and Emily was ill-prepared to handle someone like Richard Parker. But he still didn't have any evidence to condemn him, beyond his rather unethical proposal to use Garrett as bait.

Garrett glanced at his watch. He and Alvin were scheduled to meet at the Bachelor Arms to discuss their covert investigation within the hour. If he hurried, he could do a quick edit on next Tuesday's column—shopping tips for henpecked husbands—before he headed for home. He'd have the entire weekend to himself. He was looking forward to spending it in purely masculine pursuits, maybe taking in a monster truck pull or two. And staying as far away from Emily Taylor as possible.

By the time Garrett arrived at the Bachelor Arms, Alvin was waiting on the front steps, clutching a manila envelope to his chest, sandwiched between two of Garrett's nosiest neighbors.

Natasha Kuryan sat on Alvin's right, chatting amiably. The diminutive Russian-born Natasha, a former makeup artist, had an uncanny knack for ferreting out information about all the tenants in the Arms. If that wasn't bad enough, Jill Foyle sat on Alvin's left, capturing his rapt attention with her quick smile and sophisticated beauty. Between the grandmotherly Natasha and the sexy Jill, Alvin didn't have a chance. His secrets might as well be tattooed on his forehead.

"Garrett!" Natasha cried. "Here you are! We have been talking to your little friend."

"Good evening, Natasha. Jill. And what has my little friend been telling you?" Garrett asked.

"He has been telling us all about the life of an important sportswriter," Natasha said in her lilting accent.

"And whose life would that be?" Garrett asked.

Natasha waved her hand at him and chuckled. "Why, Alex's, of course. Don't you think he is quite young for such success?"

"Oh, right," Garrett said, frowning at Alvin. "You were telling them about your *successful* career. I can understand why they were impressed, *Alex*."

"Alex has also been giving us all kinds of insights into you." Jill paused and smiled sweetly. "And Emily Taylor. We didn't know you and Emily were personal friends."

"Very personal," Alvin chimed in. "Mr. McCabe took Ms. Taylor to the Farmers' Market on Wednesday and he said it was—"

"Strictly business," Garrett interrupted. "The boss told me to show Emily Taylor around Los Angeles while she was here. I'm just following orders. The same way Alex does."

Jill studied him shrewdly. "Garrett McCabe and Emily Taylor. Now there's an odd pair."

"My sentiments exactly," Garrett said.

"It makes no difference," Natasha said to Jill. "If she is the one, she is the one. Look at what happened to our Joshua and our Truman. They had no choice in the matter and now they are happily married. There was a greater power at work there."

"Well, there's no greater power at work here," Garrett assured.

"No?" Natasha asked incredulously. "You do not believe in the legend? You have not looked into the mirror?"

"No!" Garrett replied. "Now, if you ladies will excuse us, Alex and I have some business to discuss. Come on, Armstrong, I'll buy you a drink."

"Really?" Alvin said, stumbling to his feet. "You and me, going for a drink? Just like one of the guys?"

"Let's not make too much out of this. Ladies, have a nice evening."

Alvin hurried along beside Garrett as he strode toward Flynn's. The place was busy, but the big Friday night rush usually arrived after eight. Garrett waved at Eddie as he walked in, then looked for an empty booth. He found one in a quiet corner and settled Alvin in before he left to get a couple of drinks.

When he returned from the bar, Alvin was waiting for him, an anxious look on his face, the envelope still clutched to his chest. Garrett handed him the cola, then sat down. "What do you have?" Garrett asked.

Alvin gulped down the entire contents of his glass, then set it down and wiped his wrist across his mouth. He stifled a burp, then smiled. "I'm just the mule, Mr. McCabe," he said. "I don't analyze the material."

"You're the mule all right," Garrett muttered, holding out his hand. "Give me the envelope."

Alvin reluctantly handed it to him and Garrett tore the flap open. He pulled out a sheaf of memos and began to scan the text. "Has your buddy heard anything?"

"No, but he saw something. A memo from Parker to one of his lawyers. He wasn't able to get a copy, but he said it had something to do with the right to use Emily Taylor's name. And Emily Taylor's ongoing affiliation with the magazine. And the termination clauses in their employment contracts."

"What?" Garrett said. "Are you sure he read it right? Why would Parker want the magazine and not Emily Taylor? She *is* the magazine. And why would she and Nora have employment contracts with Parker?"

Alvin shrugged, gazing around the bar distractedly. "Like I said, Mr. McCabe, I'm just the mule." He leaned forward. "You know, meeting here at Flynn's makes a lot of sense. If anyone from the paper sees us, they'll just think we're a couple of good buddies out for a drink. Maybe we should scope out some babes. You know, act like this is just a normal Friday night for you. So no one gets suspicious," Alvin added.

Garrett looked up at him. "I wouldn't worry," he said. "I've never seen anyone else from the paper in here."

A forlorn look crossed Alvin's expression and Garrett couldn't help but feel a little sorry for the kid. But not nearly sorry enough to help him pick up "babes."

"Well, I gotta go anyway," Alvin said. "I've got to crunch some stats for Rowdy." Alvin stood. "You're sure I won't get into trouble for this, right?"

"Positive," Garrett said. "You've got my word on it, Alex."

Garrett watched as Alvin wove through the crowd, gaping at beautiful women as he passed. He tripped over a chair leg on his way to the door and nearly sprawled across a table, upsetting a round of drinks in the process. To Garrett's relief, Alvin finally made it to the door, leaving Garrett alone with his thoughts. He flipped through the papers again, trying to make sense of what Alvin had told him. But there was nothing there referring to a termination clause. There was, however, a rather lengthy proposal for a series of videos based on Emily's magazine, and a mention of a possible television show.

Garrett cursed in frustration. What the hell was Parker up to? It didn't make sense. Why would he want Emily out? Especially if he was planning to produce a series of—

If she can't play the game, we've made some contingency plans. If Emily Taylor isn't willing to take on the role we have in mind for her...

Parker wanted the magazine, and he had admitted wanting Emily Taylor's name. But what about Emily Taylor? She'd never agree to home videos, or personal appearances, or charity receptions, or anything that might boost her visibility. But could Parker push her out if she refused?

Garrett discounted the idea immediately. After all, she would still own a third of the magazine. And Nora owned the other third. Together they could veto any plans that Parker might have. They could get rid of Parker if they really wanted to.

Still, it would be prudent to keep an eye on the situation. He needed to find something new to report back to the sleaze. But monitoring Emily Taylor's intentions from a distance would be pretty tough. He may be forced to spend just a little more time with his favorite homemaker.

He cursed inwardly. Maybe he was just imagining problems where there weren't any. Why the hell was he so concerned about Emily Taylor, anyway? After all, she was a big girl and she could take care of herself. If she couldn't, her lawyers certainly could.

Maybe this strange need to protect her was really based in *self*-protection. Maybe he wanted her to turn down Parker's offer and go back home, taking her magazine with her. At least then he wouldn't have to deal with the strange feelings she created inside him. He had tried everything to stifle his growing attraction to her and now he was taking the next logical step—finding a way to permanently remove Emily Taylor from Los Angeles and the state of California.

But would that stop the desire that shot through him every time he thought of her? Or would it stop the overwhelming need to see her, to listen to her voice, to watch her move, to inhale the scent of her until he couldn't think straight?

For an instant, he wondered if Natasha might be right. There could be a greater force at work here, drawing him toward Emily, shaking his willpower, and turning his life inside out. He had seen the ghost, though he hadn't wanted to admit it until now. His deepest fear, his greatest dream. Emily Taylor.

He had tried to resist her, but somehow she had managed to burrow inside of his soul and capture a tiny corner of his heart. Displacing her wouldn't be easy. But he was going to have to give it his best shot.

"I'VE DECIDED not to take your advice."

Nora dragged her gaze from the photo table, a daffodil bulb clutched in her fingers. "What did you say, Em?"

"I said, I've decided *not* to take your advice," Emily repeated from the far side of the photo studio.

"I've been giving you advice since the day we met and you've been ignoring it for just as long. Which advice have you decided not to take?"

Emily wandered over to the table and picked up a freshly cut iris, then brushed it across her lips. "The advice about Garrett McCabe," Emily said.

"Was that the advice on being more aggressive?" Nora asked. "Or the self-improvement advice? Or was it the revenge advice?" Nora paused. "I do give a lot of advice, don't I? Maybe I'm in the wrong line of work. I'd make a great psychiatrist."

"I've decided I'm not going to take your advice on being more assertive. I'm just not the type of person who can go out there and take what she wants—especially when it comes to men."

"So what happened?"

"I kissed him."

Nora threw her arms around Emily and hugged her. "That's wonderful!" she cried. "I can't believe you actually kissed a man. This is a big step for you."

"Right after I hit him on the neck with a tomato," Emily continued. "And right before I ran away and locked myself in my bedroom. I've come to the conclusion that Garrett and I are not meant to spend time together. Our day at the Farmers' Market was evidence of that."

"You hit him with a tomato?"

"He deserved it," Emily said. "He was being such a jerk. He took me to the Farmers' Market to shop, so I shopped. And then he got irritated because I was spending too much time looking at vegetables."

Nora nodded in understanding. "And not enough time looking at him," she said. "That male ego really gets in the way of a good day of shopping, doesn't it?"

"Well, it showed me a thing or two about Garrett McCabe. It would take an industrial-size can opener to open up his mind. He might talk a good game, but he has no intention of trying to understand me or my readers. He's just like Eric."

"No one is just like Eric. When they made him, they destroyed the mold so they couldn't make the same blunder twice."

"Garrett McCabe comes pretty close."

"Em, if you have feelings for this man—"

Emily ran her fingers through her hair. "I don't," she said, knowing it was a lie. She had more feelings for Garrett McCabe than she'd ever care to admit. And there was the cause of all her problems.

"But you kissed him."

"Temporary insanity. Or maybe schizophrenia." She picked up a bulb and placed it closer to its flower. "Whenever I'm around him, I lose my mind. But I've regained my senses now and I'm ready to get back to work. Where did you put the crocus bulbs?" She hurried over to the line of boxes along the wall and began to search in earnest through the bags of bulbs inside.

She was learning to talk a good game, too. Though she wanted to forget everything about Garrett McCabe, she knew it wouldn't happen any time soon. After all, he was the first man in her life since her ex-slimeball. He was also the stuff that fantasies were made of. But then, considering it had been eleven years between men, any man would look good to her.

She just had to keep reminding herself that she was an absolute failure when it came to the opposite sex. Her fantasies never came close to real life. On her wedding day, she thought her marriage to Eric would be one great romance, filled with roses and champagne, soft words and lingering kisses. She was still waiting for the romance to start on the day she discovered Eric's desertion, five years later.

"Ms. Taylor?"

Startled out of her contemplation, Emily rose and brushed the dirt off her fingers, then turned to find Colin's top assistant, Becky, standing in the doorway to the reception area. A worried expression creased her brow.

"Ms. Taylor, that flower delivery man is here again," Becky said.

"That must be the guy who's delivering the extra bulbs," Nora called from across the studio. "You can send him back, Becky."

Becky walked further into the studio and let the door close behind her. "No, this is *the* delivery man," she whispered. "The one who came barging in here a few weeks back. He said you'd be expecting him."

"Garrett McCabe?" Emily asked.

"Of course we're expecting him," Nora said, rushing over to Emily's side. "Did you hear that, Em?" She clasped Emily around the shoulder and smiled smugly. "That handsome Mr. McCabe is here. Send him right back."

"No!" Emily cried, pulling away from Nora. "Don't send him back, Becky."

"Em!"

Emily pulled out of Nora's embrace. "Nora!"

"Send him back," Nora told Becky, giving her a gentle shove in the direction of the door.

"Why are you doing this?" Emily hissed.

"He made the first move. I want to see if he's come here to grovel," Nora said. The door to the studio opened and they watched Garrett walk in, a huge bouquet of flowers held over his face. "Oh, look!" Nora whispered. "How romantic. He's brought you flowers. Groveling can't be far behind."

Garrett slowly lowered the flowers and handed them to Emily, his gaze fixed on hers. "I've tried this twice before and as I remember, it didn't work. The third time's a charm, right?"

"Thank you," she said softly. "Did Mr. Parker send you again or did you come on your own?"

An uneasy look crossed his face, then quickly disappeared. "No," Garrett said. "This was my idea. I thought we might go out shopping. I'm not sure I gave it a fair chance the other day."

Emily gasped. "You want to take me shopping again?"

"Sure," Garrett said. "We can go right now. Where do you want to go?"

"I can't. I've got—"

"The Antique Guild," Nora volunteered. "Emily told me just the other day that she wanted to find some bottles to add to her bottle collection." She held out her hand to Garrett. "I'm Nora Griswold. I don't think we've ever been formally introduced. I'm Emily's business partner. I'm the one who cut up your flowers."

Garrett shook her hand. "Garrett—"

"McCabe," Nora completed. "I know. I recognize you from that pretty little photo they put next to your column. And from the bookstore."

Garrett turned to Emily. "So," he said, "you collect bottles?" A hint of disbelief colored his voice and a glazed look settled in his eyes, the same look she'd seen after a few hours of shopping at the Farmers' Market. That zombie husband look. "What kind of bottles?" he asked.

Emily smiled. "Old bottles. Any kind, really. I never know until I see one I like."

"And the guidebook says that the Antique Guild had three acres of antiques under one roof," Nora said. "Can you believe it? Three acres. Finding just the right bottle could take…days. If I were you, I'd leave right now. I'll take care of the rest of the shoot, Em. You and Mr. McCabe just run along and have some . . . *fun.*"

Emily forced back a giggle. If Garrett McCabe wasn't sorry yet, he'd certainly be sorry when Nora Griswold was done with him. Though Nora had never met Emily's ex-husband, Emily's partner had always harbored a secret revenge fantasy against Eric—a fantasy she was now transferring, or was it projecting, onto Garrett McCabe.

"Let's go then," Emily said.

Nora patted Garrett on the arm, then gave his bicep a squeeze, widening her eyes at Emily. "I'm sure you'll enjoy yourself, Mr. McCabe," she cooed. "Almost as much as I enjoy your column, I'd wager."

Garrett raised a brow in surprise. "I'm sure I will," he said warily.

Garrett followed Emily through the studio and out into the reception area. "So that's your partner," he commented. "With a partner like that, who needs a guard dog?"

"Nora can be a little overprotective," Emily said as they walked out to the street. "And a little bossy...and nosy. But she is my best friend. She's the one who had the idea for the magazine. She showed up on my doorstep one day with this proposition to turn my books into a bimonthly magazine. We went to a monthly schedule two years later and things have been going wonderfully ever since."

"Then why sell?" Garrett asked.

Emily glanced over at him. He wore a crisp oxford shirt open at the collar and a pair of pleated khaki pants that seemed to emphasize his flat stomach and narrow waist. She suddenly had the urge to see what was underneath that shirt, to see if his chest really was as muscular as it appeared. Then she realized she was staring. "Ar-Arnie Wilson, our publisher, is retiring and he wants to sell off his share of the magazine."

Garrett grabbed her hand and laced his fingers through hers, then pulled her to a stop on the sidewalk. She turned to give him a questioning look, then felt her heart stop dead as he slowly bent over and brushed a kiss across her lips. His touch was gentle, inviting, filled with tightly controlled desire. Then he smiled in his charming way and brushed an errant lock of hair from her eyes. His palm lingered for a long moment on her cheek. "I just thought we should take care of that right away," he said. "Before I spent another second thinking about it."

"You've been thinking about kissing me?" she asked, her mind swimming, her nerves humming.

He shrugged and smiled. "On occasion. But actually kissing you seems to take care of the problem. At least for a while. But don't be surprised if I kiss you again," he teased.

"I—I won't," Emily said, blushing.

He pulled her along toward his car. "You said at Parker's party that you weren't sure you wanted to sell your magazine. Have you changed your mind?"

Emily avoided looking at him altogether, disconcerted by his casual change of subject. From kissing to business in a single breath. How did he do it? She'd still be reliving the moment three weeks from now. Emily drew a deep breath and tried to focus on the subject at hand.

"I'm trying to change my mind, for Nora's sake," she said. "Nora says this is the best move for *At Home*. And having Parker's money behind us will certainly make her job easier. She's always scraping to make the budget balance. I'd like to make her life a little easier."

"Then the negotiations are going well?"

"Fine," Emily said. "Well, actually, I haven't really been involved in the negotiations. Nora's been handling that. But she says they're going fine. We have our lawyers looking everything over."

"But you're not excited about the prospect of working with Parker?" Garrett commented, opening the passenger side door for her.

Emily glanced up at him as she climbed in the convertible. "Working *for* Parker," she corrected. "Though it might look good on paper, sometimes I get the feeling that this might not be the best thing for our little magazine."

"Working *for* him?" Garrett asked. "What do you mean?"

Emily shrugged. "Nothing, really. I don't want to talk about business. It gives me a headache." The truth be told, she'd rather kiss Garrett McCabe than discuss the sale of her magazine. But she'd have to wait until he felt the urge again, because she wasn't about to throw herself into his arms the way she had after she hit him with the tomato.

"Maybe you should trust your instincts," he said.

"Or maybe I should leave the negotiations to those who know what they're doing," Emily said lightly, smoothing her skirt.

"There's a lot to be said for instinct. I believe in acting on every one of my instincts."

She shot him a sideways glance, her eyes wide.

"It's usually what makes a good businessman great," he explained with a clever smile.

"Or businesswoman," Emily corrected.

"Or businessperson, if you prefer."

"I never wanted to be a business . . . person," Emily admitted. "At first it was just the books, and then the magazine came along. There are times when I wish it was just me and my typewriter, sitting alone at my kitchen table and trying to come up with a creative new concept for holiday entertaining. Now, there are all these other things to consider, not the least of which is my image."

"Image?" Garrett asked.

She nodded. "I think Mr. Parker expects Emily Taylor to be more outgoing, more comfortable with her public, more willing to promote herself and her magazine."

"And she isn't?"

"Not this Emily Taylor," she replied. "Maybe there's another Emily Taylor out there who'd feel more comfortable in the role, but not me."

"Maybe you underestimate yourself," Garrett said.

Emily shook her head. "I don't think so. It's not just that I don't want to, it's that I can't. It's not the way I am and no matter how hard I try, I can't change how I am."

"And how are you, Emily Taylor?"

Emily bit her bottom lip and toyed with the knob on the glove compartment. "If you haven't noticed, I'm a little shy."

Garrett gasped. "No! Really? I hadn't noticed. I just thought you had naturally pink cheeks."

"It's not easy being shy," Emily said softly. "My mother used to send me to charm school every Saturday morning, hoping that it would help. I used to hide out in the bathroom until class was over and then run out and tell her how much fun I had. But I still couldn't socialize properly. Pretty soon she realized I was a lost cause and she gave up. There are so many times when I wish I was more . . . forceful."

He slid his arm along the back of her seat, then gently ran his fingers through her hair at the nape of her neck. "I think you're fine just the way you are." He smiled at her, a smile that made her feel like home-baked caramel rolls, all warm and gooey inside. She hesitantly returned his smile, then settled back in her seat as Garrett started the car.

But as his words replayed in her mind, she frowned. Certainly she'd misunderstood him. He couldn't have said what she heard. And if he had, he couldn't possibly have meant it. He liked her the way she was? How could that possibly be?

Even Emily Taylor didn't like herself the way she was.

THEY DINED ALFRESCO, on the beach, a blanket spread out on the sand, a picnic supper packed in a huge basket and hauled down the steps from the beach house. Though he had limited experience eating outdoors, the sunset and the sound of the surf seemed more romantic than the dim lighting and piped-in music of any of his favorite restaurants. As Garrett stretched his legs out in front of him and sipped at his glass of wine, he realized that it didn't get much better than this.

The picnic was a perfect end to a surprisingly pleasant day. They'd spent the afternoon searching the Antique Guild for Emily's bottles, strolling the aisles and discussing items that caught their fancy. He had to admit that the afternoon was far from the disaster he'd predicted upon hearing that they'd be shopping for old bottles.

Emily was able to chatter on and on about antiques and was a veritable encyclopedia of knowledge when it came to collecting. He'd learned a few things, seen some interesting history, and ended up purchasing an antique mechanical toy bank, exactly like one his grandfather owned, for an outrageous sum. Emily had informed him that mechanical banks were extremely collectible and that the asking price was quite reasonable. She then proceeded to negotiate the price down another ten percent before she told him he could buy it.

He'd asked her to dinner as they walked to the car and she had politely turned him down. To his consternation, she'd been quite distant from him all day long, avoiding any physical contact, even avoiding his gaze whenever possible. He was certain she still harbored some hurt feelings over their afternoon at the Farmers' Market, and his spontaneous kiss outside the photo studio hadn't seemed to help. But he was determined to put things right between them and had decided to try to kiss her goodnight when he left her at the door in an attempt to force the issue.

But when they had reached the beach house, to his surprise, she extended her own invitation for a picnic supper, then sent him off to the market in Malibu for a bottle of wine. Meanwhile, she prepared the meal and by the time he returned twenty minutes later, there was a gourmet feast waiting for them.

If he hadn't known better, he'd have suspected that she had snuck out the back door and bought takeout from one of Malibu's trendy eateries. But when she described each course of their picnic meal—chicken something-or-other, a weird kind of potato salad, and fresh fruit with a foreign name—he knew he'd probably find all the recipes in Emily's latest book, the book he'd ridiculed at the bookstore.

He also recognized many of the ingredients from the much maligned trip to the Farmers' Market. So maybe that afternoon hadn't been a total bust after all. Not if it resulted in a terrific picnic on a deserted beach with a beautiful woman.

"Would you like more potato salad?" Emily asked.

Garrett shook his head. He placed his plate beside him, then leaned back, bracing himself on his arms. The breeze fluttered at the open front of his shirt. He turned his face to the setting sun and closed his eyes. "I can't remember the last time I ate so well—or so much. But the potato salad was really good," he added.

"It's made with olive oil and fresh basil. I add ricotta and Parmesan cheese. It's an Italian version and much more interesting than your basic mayonnaise potato salad, don't you think?"

He turned to find Emily looking at him with wide green eyes, eyes he'd been drawn to from the very moment he'd met her. Their gazes locked and he felt his breath stop for an instant in his chest. Lord, she was beautiful. The setting sun glinted in her fiery hair and the ocean breeze tossed her curls into riotous disarray. He sat up, then reached out and smoothed a strand behind her ear, holding it there for a long moment, his fingertips resting on the curve of her jaw.

She used very little makeup, so all her features seemed much purer, much more touchable. His palm brushed along her cheek and he was amazed at the softness of her pale skin. He couldn't seem to quell this need to touch her. Suddenly, he didn't want to try.

She wore another of her shapeless flowered dresses, but he was beginning to believe they were the perfect choice for her. All the attention was drawn to her face, a face that radiated a powerful, yet unadorned beauty. And he liked the fact that she didn't display her body for public appreciation. Though that didn't stop his speculation about the figure beneath.

"You really enjoy what you do, don't you?" Garrett said softly.

"Yes," she replied. "But—but then I really don't know how to do anything else. Who knows, I might have enjoyed being an aerospace engineer if I'd been given the chance."

"So, how did you get started?" he said, brushing his thumb along the curve of her ear. "What made you decide to write that first book?"

She turned slightly, into his hand, as if she enjoyed his caress. "It was the only thing I could do," Emily said. "I had bills to pay and no way to pay them. I was twenty-three years old, my husband had just walked out on me, our savings were nearly gone, and I didn't want to run home to my family for help."

"Your husband was a fool," Garrett said.

"No," Emily replied, shaking her head. "I just couldn't be what he wanted. He married me when I was eighteen. I had no education past high school, no formal training. All I knew how to do was cook and decorate and garden. He needed something—or someone—more. He left me for a woman with an M.B.A. from Princeton...a woman he could talk to. She also had a big chest and long, blond hair." Emily sighed. "So you see, I haven't had much luck with men."

"I don't think one man would be considered an adequate statistical sampling," Garrett said. He slowly wove his fingers through the hair at the nape of her neck and pulled her closer. "Maybe your luck is about to change," he murmured.

He knew what he was doing was counter to every shred of common sense he possessed. This was not a kiss to tease, or to quell an urge. This kiss came from deep in his core, challenging Emily to give the same of herself. Though she was not a woman he wanted to get involved with, he couldn't stop himself. She was so sweet, so desirable. And he found her innocence refreshing and incredibly alluring.

Slowly, he lowered her back onto the blanket, watching as a myriad of emotions crossed her face—apprehension, indecision, fear and then passion. She squeezed her eyes closed as if she were afraid to look at him, and he traced her brow with his thumb, trying to wipe away the lines of tension. Suddenly, her eyes snapped open and she did look at him, her gaze wide with surprise, as if she just realized what was about to happen. In a flash, she sat up and began to fumble with the food containers scattered around them on the blanket.

"Did I mention there's Parmesan cheese in the potato salad?" Emily asked.

Garrett stifled a frustrated groan and flopped back on the blanket. Emily wasn't the only one who felt as if she were back in high school. He'd played this scene before only he'd been quite a few years younger. And as he remembered, it had been in the back seat of a Chevy Impala. "I don't want to talk about the potato salad," he said, levering himself up beside her.

"A-all right," Emily replied breathlessly. "What did you think of the grilled chicken?"

This time he placed both palms squarely on her cheeks and turned her face to his. He moved to kiss her, his lips hovering above hers, so close he could feel her quickened breath against his mouth. "I don't want to talk about the chicken, either," Garrett whispered.

"Are you going to kiss me like that again?" Emily asked, her gaze flitting from his eyes to his mouth.

"I've been thinking very seriously about it."

Her eyelids fluttered and she waited patiently, holding her breath. He brushed his mouth across hers in a simple, undemanding caress and she began to breathe again.

"I've been wanting to do that all day long," he said.

She swallowed hard. "About that—kiss . . ."

He smiled to himself. She could barely bring herself to say the word. "Which kiss?" he asked before he touched her lips with his once more. "That kiss or this kiss?" This time he ran his tongue along her lower lip before he covered his mouth with hers. She stopped breathing again and when he was certain she was about to pass out from lack of oxygen, he drew away. Her face was flushed pink and her eyes were as wide as saucers.

She cleared her throat and tried to act as if the kiss hadn't affected her at all. But he could see the hazy passion in her eyes, he could feel it in her soft lips, and he could hear it in her erratic breathing.

"The kiss from the other day," she murmured. "I—I wanted to let you know that I made a—a mistake. I didn't mean to—well, you know."

"You didn't?"

"Oh, no," she breathed. "You see, I'm not an impulsive person. And I really haven't had much experience in the area of . . ." She swallowed hard again. "Of passion," she croaked. "In fact, you're only the second man I've ever kissed in my life, not including Johnny Kelly in the second grade and that was on the cheek."

"Then you have a lot of catching up to do," Garrett said.

"Oh, no. No, I don't. You see, I've thought about this and weighed all the consequences, and I've decided that it would be best if we just remain . . . friends. I'll be leaving soon and it would be pointless for us to get involved."

Garrett drew away. This was the first time in recent memory that he'd been on the receiving end of this particular speech. If he couldn't manage to seduce a woman who hadn't been kissed in over ten years, he was definitely losing his touch. "Pointless?" Garrett asked.

She nodded nervously. "Yes, pointless."

"Is that how you really feel, Emily?" Garrett asked.

She drew a shaky breath and began to collect the utensils, arranging them neatly on a linen napkin. "I think that would be best," she said. "For both of us."

"What if I don't happen to agree?" Garrett said.

"You don't understand. I don't know how to—"

He placed his finger over her lips. "We're just kissing here, Emily. That's something that men and women do when they enjoy each other's company. I'm not asking for a lifelong commitment. We don't even have to—go steady. Friends kiss all the time."

"They do?"

He brushed his mouth across hers again. "Yes, they do."

She covered her cheeks with her palms to hide her embarrassment. "Back when I was first kissing my ex-slime—I mean, my ex-husband—I guess it meant more." She frowned. "I'm such a dope about these things. I don't know what anything means anymore. I read books, I go to the movies, but I still don't know. Somehow, I managed to miss the sexual revolution and now there's a whole different set of guidelines and no one's bothered to write them down. Nora knows them, you know them, everyone seems to know them except me."

"You'll learn them as you go along," Garrett said. "And some of them you'll just make up to suit the situation."

Emily stared at him, suspicion glinting in her eyes. "And this thing about friends kissing each other. Did you make that one up?"

"It means what you want it to mean, Emily. It means I enjoy being with you. It means thank-you for such a nice dinner. It means you have the most beautiful green eyes I've ever seen in my life."

A smile quirked the corners of her mouth. "You can be very charming, Garrett McCabe."

He pushed her down on the blanket and braced his hands on either side of her body. "You don't know the half of it, Ms. Taylor," he said before he brought his mouth down on hers.

Her hands moved to his chest and she brushed back his shirt and skimmed her fingers over his skin. A flood of desire pooled at his core, and he fought back a moan as he felt himself grow hard. He rolled on top of her and pressed himself into the soft mound between her legs.

He was a kid again, in the back seat of his best buddy's car, or lying on a stadium blanket in a quiet corner of the park, watching the sun set with his best girl. He hadn't necked with a girl since he was seventeen and he'd forgotten how treacherously arousing it was.

They spent a long time gently exploring each other's mouths. But as they lost themselves in kiss after kiss, he knew what he felt for her was more than friendship. He was a fool to think he could stop with just this. He wanted more, so much more. He wanted to touch her and feel her move beneath him, to listen to her moan and cry out his name in the heat of passion.

Garrett pulled back and looked into her apprehensive gaze, then slowly opened the top button of her dress. She watched him, wide-eyed, but she didn't make a move to stop him. He waited, then unbuttoned the next three buttons in a rush. With exquisite control, he slipped his hand beneath the fabric and cupped her breast in his palm.

Her nipple hardened against his hand and he heard her draw a sharp breath. "Is—is this what friends do?" Emily asked, turning her dusky gaze up to his.

"No, Emily," he murmured. "This is what lovers do." He bent his head over her and kissed the top of her breast, skimming the silken skin with his tongue, wanting to taste her more fully, needing to draw her into his mouth and make her moan with passion.

But then, through the heat of his desire, he felt her stiffen beneath him. She gently pushed against his shoulders.

"Don't be frightened, Em," he said, stroking her temple with his thumb, his forehead pressed against hers. "I promise, I won't hurt you. I just want to love you."

She shook her head fiercely. "No," she cried. "I can't." She rolled from beneath him and struggled to her feet, clutching at the front of her dress.

"Em, wait. I didn't mean to—"

"No. I'm sorry, but I—I just can't." She gave him an apologetic smile, then turned and raced up the beach house stairs.

It wasn't until much later, after he'd roundly cursed himself, after he'd regained a measure of control, after he'd re-packed the picnic basket and left it on her front step, that he realized he'd completely forgotten about his Tuesday night poker game. He'd never missed a Tuesday night in the year and a half that they'd played and the guys would won-der where he was.

But then again, he'd never had Emily Taylor in his arms. And that alone was enough to make a man forget his own name.

7

"THE LIQUID STUFF," Tru Hallihan said. "It always works for me."

"I use the crystal stuff and I think it's better," Josh Banks said. "It works a lot faster."

"But it can ruin the pipes, can't it?" Tru countered.

Garrett pulled out a chair at the poker table and sat down in the midst of another scintillating Tuesday night discussion. Whenever he arrived late, the topic seemed a complete mystery and tonight's discourse was no exception. He picked up the pitcher of beer and poured himself a glass. "What are we talking about?"

Tru handed the deck of cards to Garrett to cut. "Drain cleaner," he said.

"We're discussing drain cleaner?" Garrett asked in disbelief. "What prompted this discussion?"

"The theme for tonight is cleaning supplies," Eddie informed him. "We've covered furniture polish and dish soap. Last week we discussed floor wax and scouring powder. Too bad you missed it. Where were you, by the way?"

"I got tied up . . . at work." There was no way he was going to tell the guys he'd skipped last Tuesday night's poker game to spend the evening necking with Emily Taylor on the beach. Garrett had a certain image in his friends' minds and he wasn't sure how the news of his infatuation with Emily Taylor would go over. Especially after he blasted Tru and Josh for buying her book.

"Tru likes the dish soap with the built-in hand lotion," Bob continued. "But Josh says it leaves a film on the glasses. What kind of dish soap do you use, McCabe?"

Garrett gave Eddie a sideways look. "I don't know," he said. "And why would you guys care?"

"Don't you ever wash dishes?" Josh asked.

"When they're dirty, I just throw them away," Garrett said. "Why are we discussing this?"

"That doesn't seem like a very sound economic policy," Josh said. "Dishes are expensive."

"McCabe uses paper plates," Tru explained as he picked up his cards. "I used to use paper plates, too, but now, after eating off of real dishes, I wouldn't go back. Sometimes those paper plates get real soggy and the food slides right off. I used to eat standing up." He paused and stared at his cards. "Caroline doesn't let me do that anymore. You know, McCabe, you should really invest in a good set of dishes. You wouldn't be sorry."

"Then I'd spend all my time washing them. Besides, I don't use paper plates," Garrett corrected. "I use the ones made from foam."

"Bad for the environment," Eddie said.

"They melt in the microwave," Bob added.

"And they're much more expensive than paper," Josh concluded. "A set of stoneware would be much more cost effective. Taryn and I registered for stoneware. We've already received four place settings as wedding gifts."

"What do you mean you registered?" Garrett asked. "Last time I checked, dishes weren't considered deadly weapons."

"They can be when thrown by an enraged spouse," Eddie muttered, arranging his cards in his hand. They all turned to stare at him in curiosity, but Eddie just shrugged and went back to his cards.

"Wedding registration is one of the great benefits of marriage," Tru explained. "You go into a department store and you pick out all the things you want as wedding gifts, sort of like a shopping spree. Then some lady writes them all down and puts them in a computer. Your friends just call up and order something off the list. That way, you always get something you want. I put some really nice beer glasses on our list and we got a pair as a wedding gift. As soon as I have five, I'll have you guys over."

"I'll take three," Garrett said. Tru dealt him three new cards. "Why didn't you guys tell me about this registration thing?" he asked. "I spent hours shopping for your wedding gifts. You could have just printed it on the wedding invitation and made everyone's life a lot easier."

"That's the thing about registering. We're not supposed to tell," Josh said. "You're supposed to call and ask. I'll take two."

Garrett shook his head and glanced over at Bob. "It's like a secret society," he said.

"It's not so secret," Bob replied. "It's basic wedding etiquette. You can get a book on it if you want. I'll take one."

"I *don't* want," Garrett said. "This marriage stuff is too scary for me."

"Hey, don't knock it until you try it, McCabe," Tru warned.

"I should write a column on this registry thing," Garrett mused. "I was going to write my next column on flowered sheets, but I think this is better."

"What about flowered sheets?" Josh asked.

"That's how a guy really knows that his old life has been completely obliterated by a woman. He's sleeping on flowered sheets, and worse, he doesn't mind. Let's just do an informal survey here. How many of you sleep on flowered sheets?"

Eddie, Josh and Tru glanced at each other sheepishly. Flowered sheets, every one of them, Garrett thought.

"Hey, did you happen to listen to 'L.A. Live' on KTRL last night?" Eddie asked, blithely changing the subject. "They were talking about you and Emily Taylor. I haven't heard a battle like that since they discussed whether Elvis would have looked better as a blonde. It was your readers against hers, and the fireworks were flying. The quiche crowd versus the meat and potatoes brigade. Give me three."

"I wish that damn column had never been written," Garrett muttered.

"Why?" Tru asked. "Your readers loved it. Everyone's still talking about it. I saw on the news the other night that Emily's fans have been picketing the *Post*. It's great publicity for you."

"And all that publicity might just be the end of my career in greater Los Angeles."

"Taryn told me that Parker Publishing is in negotiations to buy Emily Taylor's magazine," Josh said.

"I didn't know it when I wrote the column, and now I find myself right smack in the middle of this deal. I'll be lucky if I get out alive."

"What's the problem?" Tru asked.

"Richard Parker has enlisted me as part of his 'team,'" Garrett explained. "He wants me to use any means at my disposal to convince Emily Taylor to take the deal he's offering. Any means."

"Sounds kind of slimy to me," Eddie commented.

"That's Richard Parker in a nutshell," Garrett said. "But I don't dare say that to Emily Taylor. I'm just hoping she sees the holes in Parker's character, and in his offer to buy, before she signs on the dotted line."

"But what if she doesn't?" Tru said.

"That's not an option I want to consider. Besides, she's leaning toward turning down the offer. She's not comfortable with the visibility Parker wants from her. She's real shy. Only a handful of her readers actually know what she looks like. She never does personal appearances and she isn't pictured in the magazine or in her books."

Josh tossed a chip into the pot. "As publisher of her magazine, Richard Parker would want to change that. He wants Emily Taylor and her name to be an asset, not a liability."

"He knows she's not willing," Garrett said. "I've told him that."

"Then maybe it doesn't make any difference to him."

"What if it does, though? What if he forces the issue after the purchase and she still refuses? Could he push her out?" Garrett asked.

"I guess it would depend on what he's buying," Josh replied. "Deals like these can be structured a million different ways."

"I think he's only going to own a third of the magazine. Emily would never sell him a controlling interest, especially considering the way she feels about the public part of the job."

"Then she shouldn't have anything to worry about. I'm sure her attorneys will protect her interests in the magazine," Josh said. He studied his cards for a long moment, then tossed two chips into the pot. "I raise. You know, the Emily Taylor name is what's really worth the money."

"What do you mean?" Garrett asked.

"I've seen a lot of promotional deals cross my desk, mostly with athletes and other celebrities," Josh explained. "They basically sell the rights to their name. Depending on how the deal is worded, Parker might have a clause in the contract that allows him, as publisher, to use the Emily Taylor name for promotional purposes."

Garrett shrugged. "So he puts her name in a few ads. What could that hurt?"

"There can be a lot more to promotion these days than just ads. There's product endorsements, private labeling, television shows, home videos. To be honest, compared to those, the magazine will probably be the least profitable aspect of the package. Even at a third, Parker can make a lot of money from selling Emily Taylor's name, if she lets him."

"And what if he has controlling interest?" Garrett asked.

"Then he'll make even more. Either way, if he really wants to push her out, sooner or later he'll find a way. Especially if she's an uncooperative partner."

"But her attorneys will catch any problems, right?"

"If they're smart and if they're looking at every detail. But Richard Parker didn't get where he is today without stepping on a few of the little people and cheating them out of their life savings while he was at it. Why don't you just warn her?" Josh asked.

"She'll probably decide against the deal on her own," Garrett said. "If she does, I may still be able to salvage my career."

"What if she doesn't?" Tru asked.

"I'll deal with that when the time comes. I won't let Parker take advantage of her, I can guarantee you that."

Tru watched him from over the top of his cards. "You really care about this woman, don't you?" he observed.

"I just feel like I need to . . . protect her," Garrett said. "I don't know what it is. Just something about her."

"Sort of like a little sister?" Tru asked.

Garrett considered Tru's question carefully. Any way he looked at it, he didn't think of Emily as a little sister, or any blood relative for that matter. The feelings he had for her were far from brotherly. He wanted her like no man had ever wanted a woman before. But wanting was as far as it went.

Since their night on the beach, they'd spent nearly every waking hour of the past week together—one day shopping for imported Italian dish towels for her, the next night taking in a Dodgers game for him. He couldn't think of a single thing he'd rather be doing than spending his days and evenings with her. He knew their time together might be limited and he wanted to learn everything he could about Emily Taylor.

But though they'd become incredibly close over the past week, their relationship had stalled at a chaste kiss at the front door, each one filled with unspoken yet tangible promise. To his frustration, days and evenings had not turned into nights together.

It was as if she had chosen to ignore what had happened between them on that night, as if it would conveniently disappear if she refused to acknowledge the desire. Garrett knew the feelings coursing through him would never go away completely, as long as she was near. But he also knew that if they'd gone further, if they'd made love that night, they would have irrevocably complicated things, especially when it came time for her to leave California.

Garrett sighed and raked his fingers through his hair. At least Emily had some sense, some control of all this, even if he didn't.

"So what is it, McCabe? How do you feel about Emily Taylor?"

Garrett glanced over at Tru. "I don't think of her like a little sister," he replied.

"Sounds serious," Tru commented.

He shook his head. "It's not. I mean, it can't be. She's not my type." After all, there was no way it could go any further. She wouldn't let it and neither would he. He was L.A.'s most confirmed bachelor. And she was the ultimate home-maker. And no matter what Caroline or Jill or anyone else said, opposites didn't attract, at least not for the long haul.

"Emily Taylor was born to be some lucky man's wife," Garrett said. "But not mine. I'm not interested in marriage, therefore she's not my type."

"She'd be wasted on you anyway," Tru said. "You wouldn't appreciate her."

"I'd appreciate her," Garrett countered. "In fact, I'm learning to appreciate her more each day." He chuckled to himself. "She bought me a houseplant and delivered it to my apartment."

"Garrett McCabe with a houseplant?" Tru joked. "Are you sure you can handle the responsibility?"

Garrett shot his friend an annoyed glare. "Contrary to popular belief, I'm not entirely irresponsible. I'm enjoying the plant. I look at it every day, I water it. It makes the place look more . . . homey. She also brought me a pot full of daffodils for my office desk. They look very . . . cheery."

Josh looked up from his cards. "I think you should marry her," he said bluntly.

Garrett laughed out loud. Josh made it a point to never beat around the bush, especially when he had an opinion to express. "I don't want to marry Emily Taylor," Garrett replied.

Josh blinked at him from behind his wire-rimmed glasses. "Why not?" he asked in his disturbingly direct way.

Garrett opened his mouth to reply, but an answer didn't come automatically. As he thought about it, there wasn't really any reason he *didn't* want to marry her. She was beautiful and sweet and sexy in her own special way and he could imagine living with her. All he really had were a few reasons why he *shouldn't* marry her.

He knew what was good for him. But Garrett rarely paid attention to what was good for him. He ran his fingers through his hair again then looked at his four friends gathered around the table. Good God, he'd have to come up with something better than that if he really knew what was good for him!

"Can we just get back to the card game?" Garrett said, grabbing the cards from the table and shuffling for the deal. "So, Eddie, what kind of dish soap do you use?"

A PAPER BAG flopped over the wall of Garrett's cubicle. "The sign says Do Not Feed the Columnist," she said. "But I'm experimenting with some new Christmas cookie recipes and I need a guinea pig."

Garrett turned away from his computer to find Emily peeking around the wall. A wave of pleasure washed over him as he took in her bright smile and pretty face. "I haven't had lunch yet," he said, holding out his hand.

She stepped to his desk and he reached for the bag, but Emily pulled it away with a teasing smile. "Cookies are not a proper lunch. I thought I was bringing you dessert."

"Then take me out for a nutritious lunch, Ms. Taylor," he said smoothly. "And afterward, I'll eat your cookies and I promise to tell you what a marvelous cook you are."

"Baker," she said.

"So, where would you like to take me for lunch?" Garrett asked.

A disappointed expression crossed her face. "I can't go to lunch. Nora and I have a meeting scheduled with Parker in twenty minutes."

"Then we have just enough time," Garrett replied, grabbing her hand.

"For what? Where can we get a decent, nutritious lunch in twenty minutes?"

"Just wait, Ms. Taylor. I'm about to introduce you to my kind of cuisine." He grabbed her hand and pulled her toward the elevator. "And you are about to have the best burrito in the entire country."

"I'm bringing along the cookies just in case," she said.

They headed out the front door and down the block, Garrett playfully tugging her along. "Mexican food is extremely high in fat," Emily said. "There was just a study done on it not too long ago."

Garrett laughed. "That's what makes it so good. Live a little, Emily."

"You should be eating vegetables and fruit for lunch," she countered.

"There are beans in the burritos. That's a vegetable, isn't it?"

She shook her head. "Technically, beans are a legume."

"The tortilla is made of flour. Flour is a vegetable."

"Flour is made from grain and is considered a starch, not a vegetable. That's like saying bread is a vegetable."

"All right," Garrett said. "So, I'll add some picante sauce. I *know* that's a vegetable."

Emily just shook her head and laughed. "You have a lot to learn about nutrition."

"You can teach me everything I need to know," Garrett replied. "Starting tomorrow."

They stopped in front of a brightly painted taco stand and Garrett ordered for them both. Carrying their drinks and food on a plastic tray, Garrett found a place for them at an outdoor table. Emily sat down and sipped at her drink as she watched him unwrap his burrito.

He bit into it, then held it out in front of her nose. "It's good," he teased. "Come on, give it a try."

Emily nibbled on the homemade tortilla and crinkled her nose. When it came to food, Emily definitely preferred her own recipes. He had to admit, he was starting to enjoy her cooking as well. "It's good," she said with mock enthusiasm.

"Have you ever eaten fast food?" Garrett asked.

"Not really," Emily replied. "I don't like it much. Nora took me through the drive-thru once. We ate in the car, while she was driving down the Connecticut Turnpike at eighty miles an hour. I found the concept fascinating, but the food was rather ordinary in a high-salt, high-fat way. I prefer my restaurants to come with waiters and tables and paper menus."

"Well, it's good to try new things every now and then, don't you think?" Garrett asked.

Emily giggled. "You've introduced me to more new things in a month than I've seen in the last twenty years."

Garrett grinned. "And there's more exciting things to come," he teased. "I promise."

She caught the innuendo in his comment and blushed. "We'd better get back. I'll be late for my meeting."

Garrett grabbed her uneaten burrito and stuffed it in his jacket pocket, then picked up his soda. "What's so important that you have to meet with Parker?"

"We're going to go over the final offer with all those lawyer types. They're going to answer my questions and ease my doubts," she said as they started back down the street.

Garrett frowned. "You haven't decided to go ahead with the sale, have you?" he asked.

Emily smiled ruefully. "It's been a very hard decision for me. But, yes, I've finally decided to go ahead and sell *At Home.*"

Garrett stuffed the rest of his burrito in his mouth then tossed the wrapper into a trash bin. "But you're not really selling the magazine," he said. "You're just replacing one partner with another."

"Not exactly," Emily replied.

His stomach tightened, the burrito suddenly a dead weight. He studied her warily as they walked. "What do you mean, not exactly?"

"I'm not supposed to talk about the terms of the deal," Emily said. She opened the bag of cookies still clutched in her hand. "It's confidential. Here, try one of these. They're chocolate raspberry bars and they are positively sinful." She held a cookie out in front of his mouth.

Garrett snatched the cookie from her hand and popped in into his mouth, then drew her to a stop in front of the *Post* building. "We need to talk about this," he said. "Now."

"I can't!" Emily cried, glancing at her watch. "I've got a meeting."

"So, you'll be late for the meeting," Garrett said. "You're Emily Taylor. You own the damn magazine. They're not about to start without you."

"So, what do you think of the cookies?" she asked.

Garrett shook his head in frustration. "I don't want to discuss your damn cookies. We need to talk about this deal."

"It's not a *damn* magazine and they're not *damn* cookies," she said stubbornly. "And I'm not supposed to talk about the deal. Nora said."

He followed Emily up the stairs to the front door, then grabbed her hand and pulled her back down again. "I don't care what Nora says. Tell me the truth. I thought you were selling Parker a third of the magazine."

She gazed up at him, obviously confused by his sudden concern over the details of the sale. "He wants to buy controlling interest. Nora and I will each own a twenty-four and a half percent. And we'll collect a salary as well. We'll run the creative and production departments and Parker will take over the business side."

"You're not planning to sign the deal today, are you?"

She frowned up at him, now completely bewildered by his urgent tone.

"Are you?" he demanded.

"No. We're just going over the final papers. We'll sign the deal sometime next week. What difference does it make?"

"Because I'd consider this deal very carefully before you sign." His words sounded suspiciously like a warning. He loosened his grip on her hands and forced a smile.

"I have and I think it will be best for us," Emily said. "We can't continue to operate the way we have up until now. The magazine has just gotten too big and it costs too much."

Garrett felt as if he were walking a tightrope. If Parker found out he had influenced Emily in a negative way, Garrett could kiss his job goodbye. But if he let Emily go through with the deal, he'd be worse than the snake he knew Parker to be. There was no way he could win, so he'd just have to try to salvage what he could from the wreckage.

"You know what Parker wants," Garrett said. "He wants you to become a celebrity. He wants you to get out there and sell the magazine. He's not going to be happy if you don't."

"I—I think I can handle that part of it," Emily said hopefully. "I feel much better about myself. I just have to get used to it. Besides, Parker isn't any different than any other publisher who would want to buy a share of the magazine. I'm still going to have to learn to face my fans."

"Well, I don't think you can," Garrett said bluntly.

"You—you don't?" she asked.

Garrett's heart twisted at the twinge of doubt in her voice. As far as he was concerned, Emily Taylor could do anything she set her mind to. But would she really be happy forcing herself to be someone she wasn't? He certainly didn't want to see that. "You said it yourself. *You* don't even think you can be the Emily Taylor that Richard Parker wants."

"Well, maybe I've changed my mind."

"You can change your mind, Emily, but do you really want to change the person you are inside?"

"Thanks for the vote of confidence," she said softly.

"I'm just telling you what you already know." He paused and raked his fingers through his hair, stifling the urge to shake her again. Then he reached out and placed his palm on her cheek, looking into her confused gaze. "Just promise me you won't sign anything today. Not until we've had a chance to discuss this."

"I can make this decision myself," Emily said. "I don't need you to tell me what to do."

He circled her waist with his hands and pulled her against his body, then brushed his mouth against hers. "I'm not telling you what to do," he said softly. "I care about you." He kissed her again, this time more deeply, but she refused to respond to him.

"If you care about me, stop trying to change the subject," she replied. "And stop telling me what to do."

"I'm not telling you what to do," Garrett shot back, his frustration coloring his voice again.

"Yes you are! You don't think I can handle this on my own. And you think you can distract me by kissing me. Well, I can handle this and I will. Now, I have to get back upstairs. They're waiting for me." She pulled out of his grasp and started toward the door.

"Emily," he called.

She stopped and turned around. "What?" she demanded.

"I happen to like you just the way you are," he said. "Just remember that."

His words startled her and she blinked hard. "That's exactly what my ex-husband used to tell me," she murmured.

"Dammit, Em, I'm not your ex-husband!" Garrett shouted. "You can trust me."

She stared at him for a long moment, her eyes filled with apprehension. He wanted to pull her into his arms, to protect her from Parker and anyone else in the world who could possibly hurt her. To soothe away all her self-doubt and all the hurt left over from her marriage. But right now, Emily Taylor didn't want his protection. She wanted to stand on her own.

"We'll talk about it tonight," Garrett said. "I'll pick you up at the beach house at 6:00 and we'll get some dinner. I want you to bring along a copy of the contract."

"I—I have plans for tonight. Nora and I will be having dinner together."

"We're going to discuss this, Emily. You can count on it. If not tonight, then tomorrow."

She gave him a quick nod then turned and walked back inside. Garrett bit back a vivid curse, then kicked the ground, sending a spray of pebbles into the air. There was no way he could win! He might as well go back inside and clean out his desk. If Emily mentioned anything to Parker about his concerns, he had no doubt he'd be out on his ear before the next edition went to press.

Garrett sighed disgustedly. Hell, he didn't even know why he wanted to continue working for a guy like Parker. He had never trusted him, or admired his business ethics. And he could easily find another paper who would want his column.

Boston had been after him for over a year. But the last thing he had wanted was to move back home. And Seattle had been interested at one time, but he'd heard that it rained nearly every day there.

Maybe that was the thing to do, quit before Parker had a chance to fire him. At least he'd have the satisfaction of telling the guy off. And Boston was a damn sight closer to Rhode Island than Los Angeles, California was. Garrett's breath stopped in his throat as he recognized the significance of that thought.

Was he really considering a future with Emily? He'd never been able to imagine spending his life with just one woman before. Still, if he had to, Emily would probably be his only choice. But could he make that choice—to commit himself completely to a woman?

Garrett rubbed at his eyes, then reached into his pocket for his keys. A long drive would help to clear his mind. Or a beer at Flynn's.

But by the time Garrett started his car and pulled out of the parking lot he knew exactly where he needed to go. Thankfully, the traffic on Wilshire was light and he made it home in close to record time, though he exceeded the speed limit for almost the entire trip. He swung the Mustang into his parking spot then hopped out and ran up to the front door of the Bachelor Arms.

The door to apartment 1-G was wide open when he got there. He had been prepared to knock. In fact, just a few days ago, he'd thought the spacious apartment had been rented. But as he looked inside, he realized that the place was vacant again.

Garrett slowly walked in, his eyes fixed on the mirror. This is where it had all started, with that strange vision. The woman in the pale dress, the knowing look, the enigmatic smile. From that moment on, everything had been turned upside down. First he'd met Emily and then he'd written the column and now his career, his life, was a mess.

He stared at his reflection for a long time, then reached out and touched the mirror. But nothing appeared. He scanned the ornate frame, running his hands over the finely formed pewter, before tugging on it. It was anchored securely to the wall. "Come on, sweetheart, show yourself. Prove to me I wasn't just dreaming."

When she didn't appear, he closed his eyes and tried to summon the vision he'd seen on the day Tru had moved out of 1-G. She'd had black hair and wore a simple gown. And she had smiled at him in such an odd way, as if she could read his thoughts.

"What are ya doin' in here, McCabe?"

Garrett spun around to find Ken Amberson, the building superintendent, standing in the middle of the living room, watching him with suspicious gray eyes. Though Amberson had a rather unassuming look about him— short, wiry, bald, in his midfifties—there was something kind of spooky about him as well. Garrett was nearly certain he was the source of all the wild stories about the legend.

"Nothing," Garrett said. "Just looking around. I'm surprised to find this place empty."

"There ain't been anyone livin' here since the day your buddy, Hallihan, moved out."

"But Tru told me you'd found a new tenant for this apartment," Garrett said.

Amberson's jawed jutted out. "Your friend was wrong."

"Where did this mirror come from?" Garrett said. "It was here when Tru moved in. Who does it belong to?"

"It belongs to this apartment," Amberson said.

"But who left it here?"

"Don't know. Why are you so interested?"

"Why do *you* think I'm interested?" he asked.

"I don't know that neither," Amberson replied. "Maybe you should tell me."

He shrugged. "There's nothing to tell," Garrett said.

"Then you better get outta here. I gotta lock this place up."

Garrett gave him a calculated stare, then slowly walked through the door. But as he turned around to take a last look at the mirror, the door silently swung closed. He heard the dead bolt turn. A shiver ran down his spine, and the hallway suddenly seemed cold and drafty.

He wasn't going to find out any more about the mirror, that much was certain. In fact, he'd heard more from Ken Amberson in the last few minutes than he'd heard from the guy during the whole time Garrett had lived at the Arms. And he still hadn't said anything. Ken was not a particularly forthcoming person, and he seemed even less inclined to discuss the mirror in 1-G.

Garrett glanced down at his watch. Emily's meeting would be over before long and then he'd know whether he still had a job or not. Maybe a beer at Flynn's wouldn't be such a bad idea before he went back and faced his future.

EMILY STARED AT THE DRESS in the shop window and tried to imagine herself wearing it. It was black, a color she wore only for funerals, cocktail parties and other occasions where she didn't want to be noticed. The hemline ended somewhere nearer to the waist than the knee, and the neckline suffered from the same shortage of fabric. To make matters worse, there were no sleeves. She owned more than a few pieces of lingerie that offered more coverage.

"If you like it, why don't you buy it?" Nora suggested.

Emily laughed. "It's not quite what I had in mind."

"So it doesn't have flowers on it. Let's go in and you can try it on. You'd look wonderful in it."

"Let's not," Emily replied, turning away from the window and continuing her stroll down Melrose Avenue. "I don't think I could bear the sight of my hips in that dress."

She and Nora had decided to go out on a shopping spree after their meeting with Richard Parker. After three hours of boring business talk, Emily didn't care where they went, as long as it was nowhere near any lawyers. Parker had suggested Rodeo Drive, but after she and Nora escaped his office, they had settled on a mile-long stretch of trendy shops on Melrose Avenue between LaBrea and Fairfax. They had also agreed to forget business for the rest of the afternoon.

"So, what do you need a new dress for?" Nora said. "Got a hot date with Garrett McCabe?"

"Not a date. I was thinking I'd cook him dinner, as a thank-you for dragging me all over Los Angeles. Since we're going back east right after we sign the contracts, I thought maybe I'd do it tomorrow night."

"You don't sound too excited about the prospect," Nora said.

"Of cooking him dinner?"

"No, of going back east."

Emily had to force a smile. "I'm looking forward to getting back home. I miss my gardens and my house."

"You know," Nora said, "we could always stay. This would be a great place to set up shop. You could find a house and you'd have gardens year-round. We'd be close to Parker Publishing. And Garrett McCabe lives here, too."

"That's not why I would stay," Emily said.

"Why not? You two have been spending a lot of time together. Maybe something would develop."

"We're friends," Emily said. "Good friends and that's all. He knows I'm going back east and I know he isn't interested in a permanent relationship. It's all very adult."

Nora stopped and observed her shrewdly. "Then why do you look like the little girl who just dropped her lollipop in the sandbox?"

Emily sighed. "Garrett and I had a disagreement earlier today and I'm not sure what it was all about. All I know was that it reminded me an awful lot of the one-sided conversations I used to have with my ex-husband."

"And here I was beginning to like Garrett McCabe," Nora said acerbically. "I'll have to add him to my list of slimeballs to avoid."

She shook her head. "Don't add him quite yet. I'm sure we'll be able to work this out and then everything will be fine between us."

Nora smiled and resumed their stroll. "Listen to yourself, Em. You sound so ... together, like you're actually in control of this whole thing."

"I've changed since we've come out here to California." She drew a deep breath. "I feel different, more confident. Like I can almost handle anything life throws my way. Though I'm not sure Garrett sees it that way. He thinks I need to be protected, watched over like some simpleton."

"As long as he's the one who wants to do the protecting, I wouldn't complain," Nora said.

"But I don't want him to think of me as just some helpless female. That's a person I'm trying to leave behind. He's got it in his head that I shouldn't sign the deal with Parker until he's had a chance to look at it. What is he going to tell me that our lawyers haven't?"

"Maybe it's ego," Nora suggested.

"I don't think so. I've learned to recognize his ego. It's just that our relationship is very open and honest, but I get the feeling he's not telling me something."

"You are getting to know him well, aren't you?" Nora said.

"I feel comfortable around him, like I can be myself." Emily paused, then smiled. "And he says he likes me just the way I am. I can't remember anyone who's ever really liked me just the way I am." She paused again. "And that's why I'm thinking of sleeping with him," she added in a rush.

"What?" Nora screeched, yanking her to a stop outside a New Age bookstore.

"Nothing," Emily murmured, continuing their walk at a more rapid pace.

Nora hurried to catch up. "No, I want you to repeat what you said. Just so I don't think I'm hearing voices or slipping into dementia."

"I was thinking of seducing Garrett McCabe," Emily explained.

"This is an interesting idea," Nora said excitedly. "But why McCabe?"

"For exactly the reasons I explained. I feel comfortable with him and I think that if I'm going to . . . go to bed with anyone, it should be him. He's here and I'm going back to Rhode Island at the end of next week. There won't be any messy entanglements. We're both adults. And I think I owe it to myself to sleep with one more man before I die. I don't want Eric to be the only memory I have of a sex life."

"That sounds logical," Nora commented.

"Besides, you're the one who's always preaching self-improvement. It's time I took your advice."

"Don't go blaming me for this unexpected decision," Nora said. "I was thinking more on the lines of a class or two."

"Well, I don't think they offer this particular subject in any class. I think this is what they call field research."

Nora linked her arm through Emily's and pulled her into a nearby espresso bar. "So, how do you plan to handle this seduction?" she whispered as they found a table.

"I was hoping you might be able to help me out on that," Emily said.

"Me? In case you haven't noticed, Em, I don't have a string of lovers following me around waiting for me to crook my little finger." The waitress appeared and they ordered a pair of lattes.

"But you were married," Emily said, once the waitress left.

"So were you," Nora replied.

Emily picked up a napkin and twisted it between her fingers. "Well, I never seduced my husband. I didn't have the nerve. More to the point, I didn't have the ability. You must have taken the initiative once or twice. Tell me what to do."

"I don't think you're going to want to play 'Naughty Schoolgirl and The Mean Headmaster' with Garrett McCabe." Nora smiled lazily. "And then we used to play—" She stopped, blinked, then cleared her throat in embarrassment. "Never mind."

Emily frowned. "Is that some kind of board game?"

"Not exactly," Nora replied. "Why don't you tell me what you had in mind and I'll let you know what I think?"

"Well, first I was going to make him a romantic dinner. I thought I'd do it at his place. I know he has a meeting at the *Post* late tomorrow afternoon, so I figured I'd go over to his apartment and get things ready. Then I'd be there when he got home."

"Then what?" Nora said.

"We'd eat."

"And then what?"

"That's it," Emily replied. "We'd have dinner and then we'd . . . do it. Oh, and I thought I'd bring along a bottle of wine. A few glasses might make things . . . easier."

"That's a plan," Nora said. "Not a great one, but it's definitely a start."

"So what have I missed?"

"What do you plan to say to McCabe?"

"Say? I didn't think I had to say anything. Eric and I never talked. We just—you know—proceeded."

"I think Garrett's going to want some explanation for why you're tearing his clothes off and having your way with him."

Emily felt a blush rise to her cheeks. "That's not what I was planning to do. I sort of thought I would get the ball rolling and then he'd take over."

Their coffees arrived and Nora waited until they were alone again before continuing. "That could work. But what if he doesn't take over. What will you do then?"

"Why wouldn't he take over? Men have . . . urges. Once they get aroused they can't stop themselves. My mother told me this the day before I got married." She grabbed the sugar and poured some in her coffee.

"Idiots like Eric have urges. Men like Garrett McCabe have a brain. He'll probably be as concerned about pleasing you as he is about pleasing himself."

Emily swallowed hard. "Pleasing me?" she asked.

"Of course," Nora said. "Most men these days are more sensitive about pleasing their partners."

"What if I . . . can't?" Emily asked.

"They say it's like riding a bicycle," Nora assured her. "You never really forget how."

"But what if I never learned to ride a bicycle in the first place?"

"Em, you were married. You've had sex. And you've—" Nora stopped suddenly, Emily's meaning finally sinking in. "You've never been . . . pleasured by a man?"

"Is that going to be a problem?" Emily said. "I mean, will he be able to tell? I don't want him to think I'm inexperienced. Maybe we should buy some books, so I can study the subject."

Nora took a long sip of her coffee. "Em, I think the best thing to do would be to let nature take its course. You can't learn these things from books. What happens between you and Garrett will be something unique, something special."

"Then you don't think I'm making a mistake?" Emily asked.

"Sometimes you have to follow your heart," Nora said softly. "Even when your mind still hasn't acknowledged what your heart already knows."

"And what is that?" Emily said.

"That's just another thing you'll have to figure out for yourself," Nora said with a mysterious smile. "Now what about protection? Have you taken care of that?"

Emily blinked in confusion. "You mean . . . ?"

"Exactly," Nora said.

"But isn't he supposed to take care of that?"

Nora laughed. "You *have* been out of circulation for a long time, haven't you?"

Emily attempted a smile. She just prayed it was like riding a bicycle. The only problem was, her former bicycle wasn't much of a bicycle. And faced with riding a shiny new one, she wondered if she'd be able keep herself from driving right into oncoming traffic.

8

EMILY SHIFTED the three grocery bags in her arms as she looked up at the arched front doorway of Garrett's apartment building. She'd been to the building only once, when she'd delivered his houseplant. Then, the building manager had taken the plant and personally delivered it to Garrett's apartment. But today, after ringing the manager's buzzer three times, she was beginning to think she might not find a way in.

"So much for my surprise," she muttered. And so much for the ice cream melting in one of the shopping bags. And the seafood turning botulistic. And the seduction. She'd even brought along home-baked chocolate chip cookies as a bribe for the manager, but she hadn't been prepared to get stopped at the front door.

With a frustrated sigh, she sat down on the steps to wait, shaded from the afternoon sun by a huge banana tree. The Bachelor Arms was a beautiful old building that looked as if it belonged in an old Hollywood movie. There was nothing like it in all of Rhode Island, and Emily found its Spanish architecture quite charming.

If she couldn't get in soon, she'd have to make alternate plans for the evening. She looked up and down the sidewalk one last time, then caught sight of two women approaching the building. The taller of the two was dark-haired and dressed in a sophisticated business suit. The other, more petite and blond, wore a loudly patterned smock dress and what looked like army boots.

Emily glanced down at her plain flowered dress with the white lace collar. Maybe she should have purchased something new on Melrose Avenue. Something sexier or more sophisticated, more L.A.

To Emily's surprise, the women came up the walk in front of the Bachelor Arms. The blonde smiled and spoke to her first. "Are you locked out?" she asked.

Emily returned the smile hesitantly and stood up, smoothing her dress. "Not exactly. I was hoping the manager would let me into one of the apartments. But he's not around."

She laughed, a light, uninhibited sound. "Ken Amberson is a by-the-book kind of guy. He wouldn't let the president of the United States into one of his apartments without the owner's written permission and proper identification. Who have you come to see?" she asked.

"Garrett McCabe."

"Are you Emily Taylor?" the brunette asked.

Emily glanced between the two, then nodded. How did these women know her? Could they have been at the book signing? Or were they friends of Garrett's? Oh Lord, could they be his girlfriends?

The blonde held out her hand. "I'm Taryn Wilde. I'm married to one of Garrett's friends, Josh Banks. We live in apartment 3-E."

"And I'm Caroline Hallihan. Garrett's buddy, Tru, is my husband."

Relieved, Emily shook each of their hands and smiled, this time with more confidence. After all, they seemed awfully nice, and they were acquaintances of Garrett, not total strangers.

"We were just going up to Taryn's for a cup of coffee," Caroline continued. "Would you like to come with us? You could wait there until Garrett gets back."

"I'm afraid I can't," Emily said. "Since I can't get into his apartment, I'm going to have to make some alternate plans for our . . . dinner."

"Oh, I can let you in," Taryn offered. "Garrett leaves a key inside an urn in the hall for his cleaning lady."

They each grabbed a grocery bag and walked through the front door, then down a long hallway and up a flight of stairs to apartment 2-D. As promised, Taryn produced a key that unlocked Garrett's apartment door. Emily tentatively stepped inside and looked around.

She wasn't sure what she expected, maybe something a little more . . . coordinated. Though each piece of furniture was very nice, it looked as if Garrett had decorated on the installment plan, as if he purchased furniture when he needed it, without an eye to what was already there.

Emily had never seen such an overuse of neutral colors in her life. In fact, short of the houseplant that sat in the middle of the dining room table, there was virtually no color in the apartment at all. She felt an undeniable urge to forget the seduction and redecorate, then and there.

"It's pretty grim, isn't it?" Taryn said. "I tried to give him one of my paintings but he wouldn't have it."

"This is lovely compared to Tru's bachelor digs," Caroline said. "He had a big screen television, a recliner, and books all over the place."

"Even a few colorful pillows would break the monotony," Emily said distractedly. "I'd do a slip cover for that chair in a rust or maybe a deep green. And window treatments would help soften the look a little. And then I'd get something interesting on the walls besides that beer poster. And the coffee table would definitely have to go."

"You'd better get to work, then," Caroline said, "before Garrett gets home. Start with that awful recliner my husband gave him. If you need help moving it, let us know."

Emily glanced over at her. "Oh, no! I was just—I mean, I'm not planning to—" She took a shaky breath. "This is Garrett's apartment, not mine. If he likes it this way, that's fine with me."

"Well, you could always live in your house," Taryn suggested.

Emily shook her head. "My house is in Rhode Island. Not that we'll live there. You see, Garrett and I are just friends."

"Ahh," Caroline said. "We understand." She looked over at Taryn and raised her brows. "They're just friends. Well, we should let you get to work on your dinner." The pair started for the door.

"By the way, what are you making?" Taryn asked as they stepped into the hallway.

"Seafood chardonnay in a puff pastry," Emily answered. "Braised carrots in a ginger glaze, a spinach salad with raspberry vinaigrette. And apple pie à la mode for dessert. Garrett likes pie."

"Sounds yummy," Taryn said. She waved as she walked out the door. "If you need anything, I'm right upstairs. Just give me a holler."

Caroline trailed after her. "And I'm sure we'll be seeing you again," she said.

Emily smiled as they pulled the door closed behind them. She felt a twinge of regret at their brief meeting. They wouldn't meet again, and for that, she was sorry. Caroline and Taryn didn't treat her like *the* Emily Taylor, the epitome of domestic perfection. They treated her like a—a girlfriend. She didn't have many friends beyond Nora.

With a long sigh, Emily glanced down at her watch. She had three hours to put dinner together and she still had a box and another bag in the car. Grabbing the key from the table beside the door, she headed out to the street, her stomach suddenly aflutter.

This night would be special. A lovely meal, good conversation and then . . . Emily gulped back another surge of nerves. She wouldn't think about that right now. She had a dinner to prepare. Seduction would come later.

Two hours later, she had good cause to revise her prediction for the night's success. It all began with a survey of Garrett's kitchen. She had at least expected a rudimentary complement of pots and pans and cooking utensils, so she had brought none of her own. But she was sorely disappointed. Like Mr. Hubbard, his cupboards were bare.

Undaunted, she decided that making dinner under such harsh circumstances would be a challenge. She rolled out the puff pastry with a beer bottle, stopping every few passes to pick out bits of the foil label. From there, it only got worse. For lack of a large bowl, the salad had to be mixed in a small pail she found under the sink. The only saucepan was used to boil the carrots and then make the sauce, so she was forced to use an old coffee pot to cook the seafood.

The table was set with disposable plates, a mishmash of utensils, mostly plastic, and the two wineglasses she'd brought along with the wine. The setting looked almost laughable with a lovely Irish linen tablecloth and napkins, candles in brass holders . . . and disposable dinnerware.

Almost laughable. By the time she'd slid the puff pastry into the oven on a battered pizza pan, she felt like crying. The oven took a few good kicks and a high setting to get it to heat up, but her pastries finally began to puff out properly, so she took some solace in the fact that she had triumphed over adversity. That is, until Garrett walked in the door and all her confidence disappeared.

Emily smoothed her frazzled hair, then clenched her skirt in her fists and watched from the doorway of the kitchen as he tossed his keys on the table near the door. He turned and saw her, and his eyes widened in surprise.

"Emily, what are you doing here? I tried to call you from the office, but Nora told me you were out for the evening."

She pasted a tight smile on her face. "I—I'm making you dinner," she said, trying to keep her nerves from overwhelming her voice. "I wanted to thank you for showing me around L.A."

Garrett smiled. "Dinner?"

"Seafood chardonnay in puff pastry," Emily said. "And pie for dessert."

He sniffed the air and nodded. "It smells good."

She took a nervous step toward him. "It—it was quite a challenge to put together a dinner in that kitchen," she said. "You have nothing to cook with. A good set of aluminum cookware and some everyday stoneware might be a sensible purchase. And maybe a few utensils, too."

He walked across the room and kissed her on the forehead. "I guess we'll have to go shopping again," he murmured, his lips warm against her skin. "In fact, maybe I should consider registering."

A shiver of apprehension skimmed down her spine at his touch. Slowly, she gathered her courage and wrapped her arms around his neck, then pushed up on her toes and pressed her mouth to his.

What began with doubt ended in a long, slow, delicious kiss, filled with desire. She shocked herself with her sudden streak of boldness. And she must have shocked Garrett, too, because when it was over, he pulled back and looked down into her eyes, studying her, as if trying to read her mind and her intentions. She smiled and ran her fingers lightly through his hair.

He lowered his head again, this time probing, testing her limits with his tongue, putting his body and soul into the kiss. She'd never, ever been kissed in such an intensely thorough way and she wondered how she could have called anything she'd experienced in the past a real kiss. Dizzy, she matched his actions, running her tongue tentatively along his lower lip, wanting to learn more from him. The experiment went on, Garrett testing, Emily trying, both of them tasting the passion that had been dormant since their night on the beach.

"I'm starting to enjoy this dinner," Garrett murmured against her neck.

"Oh," she breathed. "I forgot about dinner. I'd better . . ."

Garrett's mouth came down on hers again, stopping all further thought of cooking, and all further thought of breathing and thinking, and standing upright. "This is different," he said, his lips still touching hers as he spoke. "Why is it different, Em? I thought we'd both decided not to go any further."

"I—I changed my mind," she replied.

A smile curved his firm mouth and lit up his eyes. "Are you sure?"

She nodded, gnawing on her lower lip. "We're adults. We can make our own rules," Emily explained.

His fingers skimmed along her jawline. "Yes, we are adults."

Emily drew in a long breath as she stared at him. "Yes—we are." Lord, he had to be the most handsome man she'd ever known. She could spend hours looking into those pale blue eyes, running her hands through his silky sun-drenched hair. "Would you like some wine?"

Garrett rubbed her upper arms and smiled. "I'd love a glass of wine."

Emily hurried to the kitchen, grateful for a chance to collect her thoughts. This was going well. Much better than she could have anticipated. All she had to do was keep her wits about her and pretend she knew what she was doing.

She rummaged through the drawers in search of a cork-screw, before she realized she had brought one along. After four attempts, she finally managed to get the cork out of the bottle, then sloshed enough wine into a glass before she gulped it down. She filled both glasses before the bottle slipped out of her hand and crashed into the sink. The rest of her courage washed down the drain in a mess of splintered green glass.

"Is everything all right in there?" Garrett called.

"Just fine," she replied.

Emily returned to find Garrett on the couch. Sitting down next to him, she gave him a glass of wine with a shaky hand. "How was work today?" The words were barely out of her mouth before she realized what a cliché they were. She fought back a blush and took another big swallow of her wine.

Garrett rested his arm on the back of the couch and toyed with the curls that brushed her temple. Though she could recall him touching her in such a way before, it felt suddenly more intimate, more meaningful.

"Fine," he said.

"I—I'm sorry about our argument yesterday," she said. "I brought the contract along and I thought we could—"

"Let's not talk about that now," he murmured. He placed his wineglass on the coffee table and then grabbed hers and set it beside his. Cupping her face in his hands, he kissed her again, deeply, his tongue invading the moist recesses of her mouth.

She surrendered to his kiss and all the passion it triggered. She'd made the right decision, to choose this man. But could she go further? Could she take the next step? She reached up and clasped his hand in hers, then slowly drew it downward, toward her breast.

Hesitating for a split second, she opened her eyes and looked at him through a haze of desire. She drew a deep breath, wanting, needing his touch on her body. Then she realized the haze was not desire. She sniffed the air. "Is—is something burning?" she asked.

"Definitely," Garrett moaned. "And I'm pretty sure it's me." He pushed her back on the couch, stretching over top of her, lacing her fingers in his and pressing her arms up over her head.

Emily untangled her hands and pushed against his chest, then twisted from beneath him. "No. I think something really is burning." She jumped up and raced to the kitchen, straightening her dress along the way. Smoke poured out of the oven. With a cry of alarm, she grabbed the door and pulled it open, but she had no pot holder, nothing with which to remove her ruined pastry shells.

"I can't get them out!" she cried. "It's too hot. Don't you have an oven mitt?"

Garrett frantically rummaged through the kitchen. "I don't use the oven. The thermostat is broken."

"You don't have a working oven?" Emily shrieked. "How can you not have a working oven? It's like indoor plumbing. It's a basic necessity."

Finally, Garrett ran for the bathroom and returned with a bath towel, wadded it up and pulled the pizza pan from the oven. The pastry shells looked like hockey pucks, black and hard and totally inedible. Garrett picked one up and tossed it against the counter. "Are these supposed to be so dark?"

"No!" Emily said.

He shrugged. "Oh. I thought you might be making one of those Cajun recipes."

Emily groaned then covered her face with her hands. Tears burned at the corners of her eyes and slipped down her cheeks. "I wanted this to be so nice," she sobbed. "And now it's all ruined."

"It is nice, Em," Garrett said, prying her fingers apart.

She dropped her hands to her side. "No, it isn't! It isn't nice at all." A laugh struggled to break through her tears. "I wanted to make a romantic dinner. And then, I—I was going to seduce you." Suddenly, her laughter took on a hysterical tone. "Can you believe it? I was worried about the seduction part, but I can't even get the dinner right. I must have been crazy. I don't have any idea what I'm doing."

Garrett spanned her waist with his hands and kissed her wet cheeks. "I'm really not that hungry," he said. He tipped her chin up until she looked into his gaze, his brow quirking up with suppressed humor. "I ate a late lunch."

She blinked back her tears and watched him warily. "You did?"

He nodded and kissed her on the top of the head. Then, clasping her waist, he lifted her up on the counter. He stepped between her legs and held her hands in his. "Forget about dinner," he murmured, placing her fingers on his chest. "Seduce me, Emily."

She gulped. "Really?"

He ran his hands up her thighs, then pulled her toward him. "Really."

She felt her face flame. "I'm not sure I know how."

"I'll help you along. Why don't you start by unbuttoning my shirt."

With fumbling fingers, she worked at the buttons, one by one, each one giving her more confidence. When she finished, she pushed his shirt open and placed her palms on his smooth, muscular chest. She could feel his heart thud beneath her right hand, slow and easy, so different from her racing pulse.

He held out his wrist and she undid the cuffs before he shrugged the shirt off his shoulders and it dropped to the kitchen floor. Her hands splayed over his warm skin and he sucked in his breath and closed his eyes at her touch. Slowly, she explored the contours of his body, the sharp angle of his collarbone, the strong line of his shoulders and the rippled muscles of his stomach. She'd never touched a man like this, with such delicious leisure and open admiration. His body was perfect in every way, strong and hard, overpowering in its beauty.

"Unbutton your dress," he murmured, watching her through half-shuttered eyes.

She shook her head. "You do it for me," she ordered, amazed at her uncharacteristic nerve.

He grinned and languidly worked his way from her collar to her hemline, pausing after each button to explore what it revealed. Soon, her dress slipped off her shoulders and puddled around her on the counter, leaving her in just her slip and underwear. She slowly released the breath she held.

"Shouldn't we go to the bedroom now?" she asked.

Garrett shook his head. "I want you right here."

She'd never made love in the kitchen before. In fact, she'd never made love anywhere except under the covers in a darkened bedroom. But the notion of it sounded wicked and uninhibited. It should be different with Garrett, she thought to herself. She would remember it more vividly that way.

"The kitchen would be fine," she replied.

He chuckled, then slid his fingers under the straps of her slip and pulled them down over her shoulders. He took in her every expression, absorbing her desire into his gaze, his own need smouldering in his eyes, carefully banked, waiting. Though apprehension shot through her at every move, she made no attempt to stop him. This was what she wanted, this and so much more. And Garrett was the man

who would give it to her, who would make her feel like a
real woman.

He smiled and rubbed a slip strap between his thumb and
middle finger. "White," he said with a chuckle. "I guess I'll
have to rethink my underwear theory."

Skimming his hands over the lace and silk, he caressed
her breasts. She held back a moan, but then he bent to capture a hard bud in his mouth, teasing at it through the damp
fabric. Her eyes widened and the moan died in her throat
as wave after wave of pleasure washed over her. There was
no doubt in her mind that he had done this before, but she
had to admit that in Garrett's case, practice had made perfect.

It was as if he opened a floodgate with his touch. Suddenly, she wanted something more, but she wasn't sure what
it was. A nagging knot of anticipation twisted at her core
and she ran her fingers through his hair and pressed him into
the soft mound of her breast, the tension growing even more
unbearable.

His lips branded her skin, hot and demanding, blazing a
trail of liquid heat from her nipple to her mouth. "I want
you, Em," he murmured, against her cheek. "Let me love
you."

His gaze locked on hers and she nodded, unable to reply.
Love me, her mind urged, forming the words she couldn't
say. Love me long and hard, love me until I can't remember
making love to any man before. Love me so I'll never want
another man for the rest of my life.

He turned and circled her ankle with his warm fingers,
then pressed a gentle kiss in the arch of her foot, slowly
working his way up her leg, teasing with his tongue, biting,
caressing. She closed her eyes and focused on the touch of
his warm mouth. Somehow, she had lost control of the situation and he had become the seducer and she, the sedu-

cee. But she didn't care. Right now, all she cared about was the erotic path his mouth was making up her leg.

When he reached her knee, he bunched her slip in his fists and pushed it up around her hips, then continued on, brushing his tongue along her thigh. She knew he wouldn't stop there and she didn't want him to. He would be the first to love her in this strangely forbidden way. She threw back her head and braced her hands on his shoulders, losing herself in the sensations, the anticipation, the need.

Slowly, he pulled the damp fabric of her panties aside. And then he touched her, first with his fingers and then with his tongue, sending a shock wave reverberating through her body. Every inhibition she ever possessed dissolved under his onslaught and she heard herself cry out, first in surprise and then, moaning his name.

Clenching his hair in her fists, she pressed him closer and the knot within her twisted tighter. She felt as if she would die if the tension didn't break soon and she urged him on with soft, wordless invocations. Every nerve in her body hummed with the tension and her mind could focus on nothing but the feel of him between her legs.

And then it came, suddenly, sending a tidal wave roaring over her, flooding her senses, tossing her about, stealing her breath until she could do nothing more than release her body to its whims. No other man had ever brought her to this place. And this was what she would share forever with Garrett, this explosion of passion and power, this surrender of heart and mind and body.

When the haze had cleared and she opened her eyes, he was still there, watching her and waiting. Suddenly buoyed by the realization of her own sexual power, Emily reached down and unbuckled his belt. With deliberate leisure, she dispatched the button and then his zipper. But Garrett grabbed her wrist to halt her progress. He ground his teeth, as if trying to maintain some shred of control. "If you touch me, Em, there's no going back."

Her gaze locked on his and she tugged her hand out of his grip. Slowly, she ran her fingers along his hardened shaft, the silk of his boxers enhancing her touch. He cupped her face in his palms and kissed her, frantic, as if trying to divert his mind from her ministrations. The need surged anew and they tore at each other's clothes until nothing remained between them but skin.

He murmured her name, nearly incoherent now, and she knew he could wait no longer. She rummaged through the grocery bags on the counter, finding the protection she'd purchased. He watched her, his jaw clenched, as she tore open the foil packet and clumsily sheathed him. Then he closed his eyes and let go of a tightly held breath.

Slowly, she drew him toward her, guiding him to her moist entrance. With exquisite care, he entered her, hard and sure, filling her until she ached. It was then, as he moved inside her, as she listened to his harsh breathing and his soft moans, that she realized this was the way it was supposed to be between a man and a woman. This sharing of needs, this uninhibited exploration of boundaries and limits and peaks of desire. And it was then that she realized she had never really made love to a man before. He was her first.

Later, after they had made love again in his bed, she fell asleep in his arms, knowing a complete and utter sense of satisfaction and fulfillment. This was what should have been all those years ago and this was who she should have had. Not the man she married, but this man who made her senses soar and her heart sing. This Garrett McCabe.

EMILY SLOWLY OPENED her eyes to the bright morning light. She held herself absolutely still, blinking as her sleep-muddled mind cleared. Her gaze flitted around the room while she tried to gain her bearings. Where was she? This wasn't her bedroom at home, or the room at the beach house. She reached out and ran a hand over the rumpled sheets on the empty side of the bed.

"Morning, sleepyhead."

Slowly, she rolled over to find Garrett McCabe standing next to the bed, dressed only in a pair of jeans, unbuttoned at the waist. Oh, Lord, now she remembered. She was in *his* bed. And she was naked and he was dressed. It was now the morning after. And she had absolutely no idea what the protocol was for extracting herself from this particular situation.

"I thought I'd run down to the coffee shop and get us some breakfast and the morning paper," he said, finishing up the buttons on his jeans and slipping into a pair of battered deck shoes.

Emily clutched the sheets around her neck and stifled a sigh of relief. So this was how it was done. He would leave and allow her to compose herself and get dressed. "That would be . . . nice."

He pulled on a T-shirt, then bent over the bed and kissed her on the forehead. She felt a surge of desire rush through her at the simple touch of his lips and she tried to stem a flood of pure affection for him. She wanted to reach up and pull him back into bed, to keep the realities of the outside world from interfering in what they'd shared the night before. But she didn't.

He walked to the bedroom door. "Don't go anywhere, Em. We have some things to discuss when I get back."

"Discuss?" she croaked. "We're going to . . . discuss it?"

Garrett chuckled and raised his brows. "Well, maybe not right away," he teased. "We may get distracted again. I'll be back in ten or fifteen minutes. Why don't you pull those covers up over your head and get some more sleep."

Emily watched him walk out of the bedroom, then listened for the sound of the door closing behind him. Was this normal, to rehash the whole thing the morning after? With a yelp of alarm, she yanked the sheet off the bed, wrapped it around her naked body, and raced into the kitchen. Her clothes were all there, scattered over the countertops and the floor, among the burnt pastry puffs and the remnants of last night's attempted dinner.

She dropped the sheet where she stood and tugged her clothes on. When she was fully dressed, she stood in the middle of the kitchen and closed her eyes, bracing her arms on the edge of the counter and drawing a deep breath. It was then that it hit her, like a blow to the stomach, knocking the wind right out of her and causing her eyes to water with the pain.

What had she done?

This was supposed to be so easy, so practical. After all, they were adults and they made their own rules. This was only supposed to be a lesson in self-improvement. She would seduce him and then leave. But the feelings that raced through her were so intense, so overwhelming, that she felt paralyzed, unable to move. She didn't want to walk out, to leave him behind as just a pleasant memory, an experience from the past. And she didn't want the memory of him, standing at the bedroom door, a sweet smile on his face, to be her last.

She wanted to make love to him again and again. She wanted to go to bed with him at night and wake up with him in the morning. And she wanted to care for him, to make a home for him, to have his children and grow old together with him. Everything she'd wanted for her life, she now wanted with him.

Denying her feelings was no longer possible. She'd hidden them away in a dark, secret corner of her heart, refusing to acknowledge that they were there, and that they were growing. She'd known from the start that there could be no future between them. He didn't want marriage, or even a committed relationship. He was L.A.'s most confirmed bachelor and his career hinged on remaining single.

And she couldn't take the risk, couldn't give her heart to a man that might shatter it again into a thousand irreparable pieces. It was already too fragile, too scarred by her past to survive even the slightest tremor.

So she was faced with the only decision she could make. She would leave, put herself as far away from Garrett McCabe as she could. And she would give herself no opportunity to see him again. A tear traced its way down her cheek and she brushed it aside and steeled her resolve.

With a shaky sigh, she turned and grabbed her car keys from the counter. Then she walked over to the couch, sat down and reached for the phone. Emily dialed the beach house number and waited for Nora to answer. Her friend picked up after six rings.

Nora's voice was raspy and muddled by sleep, but still calming to her jangled nerves. "Hello?"

"Nora? It's me. I'm sorry if I woke you."

"Em?"

"Nora, I need you to do something for me. Are you awake? Are you listening?"

A groan was the only reply.

"I want you to call Richard Parker and tell him that you and I will meet him and his lawyer at his office in three hours. Then call our lawyer and tell him to meet us there, too. Then I want you to call the airline and get us tickets back to the east coast for early this afternoon. Do you have all that?"

"Em, what happened last night?"

"Everything," she said, trying to steady her voice. "Now are you sure you got it all? I'll be back at the beach house within the hour to pick you up. Have your things packed. I want to leave for the airport as soon as the meeting is over. It's time to put this deal to bed."

"Em, what's wrong?" She could hear the concern in Nora's voice and she wanted to tell her everything. But there was no time.

Emily blinked back a flood of tears and told only what was necessary. "I—I think I'm in love with Garrett Mc-Cabe."

GARRETT STROLLED down the street, munching on a donut and reading the morning paper, Emily's breakfast tucked under his arm. He almost felt like whistling and he couldn't recall ever whistling before. In one short, twenty-four-hour stretch, his life had taken a definite turn for the better.

It was hard to believe that less than a month ago, he had considered himself a happily unmarried man, steadfastly single, a confirmed bachelor. And now, he had Emily. Beautiful, sweet, sexy Emily. Suddenly he knew why he'd waited so long. He had been waiting for her, knowing that she was out there somewhere.

It scared the hell out of him that he'd almost let her get away. If it hadn't been for last night, he never would have acknowledged how he really felt about her. And she would have gone back to Rhode Island, back to a life that didn't include him.

His choice was obvious now. He'd quit the *Post* and go back east with her. Maybe he'd try to get that job in Boston and try the syndication deal again. Or maybe he'd just take a break and enjoy Emily's company for a good long time. And then, when the time was right, he'd marry her.

As he stopped on the top step of the Bachelor Arms and fumbled for his keys, he glanced over at the brass plaque that identified the building in block letters. He had looked at the sign hundreds of times before, but he'd never noticed the graffiti scrawled beneath it.

Believe the Legend.

Garrett laughed. Maybe there was something to it. After all, who would have ever thought he'd actually be thinking of marriage? At one time, it was his deepest fear. And now, maybe it was his greatest dream.

As he walked through the hallway to his apartment door, he heard his phone ringing. Shoving the key into the lock, he pushed the door open, then dropped everything on the small table beside the door. He picked up the receiver and brought it to his ear. But before he could say hello, the voice on the other end of the line cut him short.

"The team bus leaves at dawn."

Garrett frowned. "Alvin, is that you?"

"Alex!" came the loud reply.

Garrett pulled the receiver away from his ear. "All right, Alex. Why are you calling me at home? Where are you?"

Alvin's voice suddenly lowered to a whisper. "I'm at work. I think you better get in here."

Garrett laughed. "No way. There's nothing that's going to get me into work this morning, Alex. Wild horses couldn't drag me out of this apartment right now."

"They're going to sign the deal this morning. In about three hours. Word just came down from the top."

"That's impossible," Garrett said. "They can't sign the deal without Emily."

"She's the one who called the meeting, Mr. McCabe."

"*What?* When?"

"Ten minutes ago. My buddy says Parker got a call from Nora Griswold telling him that Emily Taylor was ready to sign. He's supposed to have his lawyers here at eleven."

"Your buddy in the mail room has got his wires crossed, Alvin. When he gets the story straight, give me a call. But don't count on reaching me this morning. The phone's going to be off the hook."

Garrett hung the phone up, then unclipped the line from the back. Nothing would disturb them, not even Alvin and his secret agent fantasies. They'd have some breakfast, then crawl back under the covers and make love for the rest of the morning.

He grabbed the bag and walked toward the bedroom. "Em? I brought you coffee. And the paper." He turned into the bedroom. "Em? Are you awake?" The sight of the empty bed stopped him in his tracks. "Em?" He looked in the bathroom but she wasn't there. It was only when he wandered into the kitchen and found her clothes gone that he realized she was gone, too.

"Damn," he muttered as he stared at the bedsheet on the kitchen floor. Alvin couldn't be right, could he? She wouldn't have agreed to sign the deal, not until after they'd talked. What could have possessed her to call and have Parker move the signing up an entire week?

Unless . . . Unless she was feeling half of what he was feeling. Maybe she'd decided that this was the only way they could be together, if she'd sign the deal with Parker and move her business to California. Garrett groaned. She was about to make the biggest professional mistake of her life and he was the cause.

"Why didn't we talk about this last night when she wanted to?" he muttered to himself. Because all he could think about then was making love to her, that's why. He didn't want to talk business any more than she did.

So, what the hell was he supposed to do? He didn't have any proof that Parker was locking her into a crooked deal. Maybe he wasn't. Hell, maybe it was even for the best.

When she signed, he'd keep his job and she'd relocate to California. On the surface it seemed like a perfect solution. But there was much more lurking just below the surface. Like a shark named Richard Parker.

Garrett glanced around the kitchen, then grabbed an empty grocery bag and looked inside. She'd told him last night that she'd brought along a copy of the sales contract. In her rush to leave, maybe she'd left it behind. He found the contract on the counter next to the refrigerator, under another grocery bag. Glancing at his watch, he estimated he had a little over an hour to figure out just what Richard Parker had planned for Emily Taylor and *At Home.*

After only five minutes of struggling through the legalese, he realized that he couldn't understand the contract without a translator. And there was only one translator he could find on such short notice. He grabbed his keys and hurried to the door. If he was lucky, he could catch Josh before he left for work.

At his knock, Taryn opened their apartment door. Her hair was rumpled and she still wore her robe. "Hi, McCabe. What's up?"

"Is Josh still here?"

She nodded then turned away from the door. "Josh?" she called. "Garrett is here." She stepped back from the door. "He's getting dressed for work. Why don't you come in and sit down and I'll get you a cup of coffee?"

Garrett stalked inside, but he couldn't sit down. The clock was ticking. He paced back and forth through the living room, twisting the contract in his hands and trying to remain calm.

Josh appeared a few moments later, dressed in his usual suit and tie. "What's going on, McCabe?"

Garrett held the contract out to him. "I need your help," he said. "I need you to find me the reason why Emily shouldn't sign the deal with Parker Publishing. And I need you to find it quick."

9

"ARE THEY IN THERE?" Garrett demanded, striding past Richard Parker's secretary.

"You can't go in!" she cried. "Mr. McCabe, come back here. That's a private meeting." She scurried after him and made a halfhearted attempt to grab his arm, but he slipped out of her grasp and flung the door open. It crashed against the wall, rattling the pictures and awards that hung there.

The five people in Parker's office turned at the commotion. Emily, Nora, Richard Parker, and the two lawyers all stared at him with undisguised shock. Garrett fixed an unwavering gaze on Emily and felt his pulse quicken. Her cheeks were flushed and her eyes bright. Tension subtly lined her face. She looked tired and upset, not happy at all. He fought an impulse to go to her and pull her into his arms, but something in her manner told him to wait.

"I'm sorry, sir," Parker's secretary said, pushing by him. "I tried to stop him, but—"

"Never mind." Parker regarded Garrett with cold eyes, then waved his secretary off. "Let him in. Maybe he can explain what's going on."

"But—but he has nothing to do with this," Emily said, averting her gaze from Garrett's. "This is my decision."

Garrett took another step into the room. "Em, we need to talk."

"Well, well," Parker said. "Don't you think it's a little too late for talking now, McCabe?"

"Maybe you should talk to him, Emily," Nora murmured.

One of the lawyers cleared his throat. "I wouldn't recommend talking to anyone right now, Ms. Taylor. At least, not without your lawyer present."

"I'm not going to talk to him. He has nothing to do with this," she repeated calmly. "This is my decision and whatever he has to say won't change my mind."

Garrett captured her gaze again and held it. "Emily, I'm not telling you what to do," he said. "I'd never do that. But I do care about you. And you didn't know all the things you should have before you signed those papers."

"I certainly underestimated your talents, McCabe," Parker said. "I thought you'd be the one to convince Ms. Taylor to put her trust in Parker Publishing. I thought you were a team player."

"A team player?" Emily said, glancing at Parker. "I don't understand. What does Garrett have to do with the sale of *At Home?*"

Garrett laughed bitterly. "Thanks to Parker, I'm caught right in the middle of this."

"How?"

"You don't know the kind of man Richard Parker is, Em. And you don't know to what lengths he went to get you to sign that contract."

Parker leaned back in his chair and kicked his feet up on his desk. "Please illuminate us all, McCabe. I'm very interested in hearing what you have to say about the person who signs *your* paycheck."

"I'd like to speak to Emily in private," Garrett said. "Em, come on. Let's get out of here. Take that contract and tear it up."

Her lawyer stood up. "As I said before, Ms. Taylor should not speak with—"

"Enough!" Garrett shouted. "She'll talk to me. Alone."

Emily shook her head. "I'm not leaving here," she said. "Whatever you have to say, you can say it front of all of us."

"All right," Garrett replied. "Here it is. Parker was a little worried that you might not agree to the sale. So he decided to improve his chances. He decided to use me to push this deal through."

Her brow furrowed in confusion. "Use you? How?"

"He wanted me to . . ." Garrett turned to Parker. "How did you put it?" He looked back to Emily. "He wanted me to romance you," Garrett said bluntly. "And then he wanted me to report back to him, to tell him everything you said about the deal. And he made it very clear that my job was on the line if I didn't agree."

"That's a lie," Parker replied, his tone deceptively believable.

"Did you?" Emily asked softly.

Garrett shook his head. "I never told him anything that he didn't already know. And I told him a lot more that wasn't true."

"That's not what I meant," she said in a timid voice. "Is— is that why you spent so much time with me? So you could convince me to sign the deal? So you wouldn't lose your job?"

"No!" Garrett said angrily. "You know how I feel about this deal. And I don't give a damn about my job."

Emily watched him, a growing suspicion in her eyes. "I don't believe you," she said. "This was all part of a plan." She glanced over at Parker. "The column, the apology, all the time we spent together? And I never would have suspected, especially after the way this all started. You both thought I was some naive little housewife, so gullible, so easy to manipulate."

"Em, you know that's not true," Garrett said. "I never once tried to convince you to sign the deal. In fact, I've been trying like hell to talk you out of it."

"Is *that* true?" Nora asked, grabbing Emily's arm. "Is *he* the one who convinced you to kill the deal?"

Garrett gasped, staring at Emily in utter surprise. "You killed the deal?" he asked. "You mean, you *didn't* sign?"

"And you've been working against us, McCabe," Parker said smugly. "I'd say that was a rather blatant admission of guilt."

Garrett turned to Parker and laughed. "Yeah. I've been working against you. You're the last person Emily should sell to. You don't want her, you want her name and what you can make from it. You're slime, Parker, and it's time everyone in this room knew it."

A transparent smile twisted Parker's mouth. "And you're—"

"Don't say it," Garrett interrupted, holding up his hand to silence the man. "I quit."

"You're fired!" Parker shouted.

"Oh, no," Garrett replied. "I quit. I'm not going to give you the satisfaction of firing me." He strode over to Parker's desk and picked up a sheaf of papers, then turned to Emily. "Is this the contract?"

She nodded, wide-eyed.

Garrett tore it in half and tossed it back on Parker's desk. "Now, if you'll excuse us, I have a few things to discuss with Ms. Taylor before I clean out my desk. Don't worry, I'll be out within the hour." Garrett turned and strode over to Emily, then grabbed her hand and pulled her out of the chair.

"You'll never work in this town again, McCabe," Parker shouted. "And you just walked out on the best deal of your life, Ms. Taylor. Give it a year. The only place you'll be able to find your magazine is on the bottom of a birdcage."

Emily turned back and looked at Parker, a worried expression on her face, but Garrett pulled her out of the office and shut the door behind him.

"Maybe he's right," Emily said softly. "Maybe I am making a mistake by not signing the deal."

"He's blowing smoke, Em," he said, pulling her inside an empty conference room. "You did the right thing. Sooner or later Parker would have destroyed your magazine, the same way he's destroyed a lot of others. In a few years, you wouldn't even have recognized *At Home*. You and Nora probably wouldn't have even been a part of it any more."

Emily pulled out of his grasp. "Why didn't you just tell me?"

"I was planning to this morning over breakfast. That's why I asked you to bring the contract along. But when I got back you were gone."

"But what about earlier? You could have said something earlier."

"I didn't know for sure until I had a chance to see the sales contract. And even then I didn't know what the hell I was reading. I had to take it to Josh for a translation. He's the one who said you had cause to be suspicious."

Emily crossed her arms beneath her breasts and tipped her chin up stubbornly. "Well, you didn't have to barge in and save me like some white knight. I'm perfectly capable of making decisions for myself. I knew something wasn't right," she said uneasily, "so I refused the offer. I didn't need you to tell me what to do."

"Em, I care about you," Garrett said, pulling her into his arms.

She stiffened her spine and stepped back. "Thank you for your concern, but as you can see, everything turned out just fine."

"What's wrong?" Garrett asked, frowning.

"Nothing," Emily said.

"Then why don't we go pack your things from the beach house before Parker has them thrown out on the street," Garrett suggested. "You can stay with me until you're ready to go back home. We'll go out this afternoon and buy some pots and pans. In fact, we'll equip my whole kitchen. And after that, you can teach me to cook."

Emily fixed her gaze on a point somewhere over his shoulder. She swallowed hard and blinked nervously. "Nora and I are flying back east today. Our plane leaves in another two hours."

Garrett grabbed her chin and turned her eyes to his. "Why? Why would you leave now when everything is finally coming together for us?"

She cleared her throat and shrugged in careful nonchalance. "Just because we...slept together last night, does not mean we have a future together. We're both adults. We make our own rules."

Garrett laughed. "Come on, Em. Don't tease me like that. That's not the way you feel. I was there last night and something special happened between us. You can't deny it."

"So it was nice," she shot back. "I'm not saying it wasn't nice."

"Why did you let me make love to you, Em, if you didn't feel something?"

"Self-improvement," she said, raising her chin defiantly. "I wanted to see if I remembered how."

"I don't believe you," Garrett said, grabbing her shoulders and giving her a gentle shake. "Tell me the truth."

She drew in a deep breath. "The truth is that I've been married once before and it was not an experience I'd care to repeat. I'm not good at permanent relationships and I'm not willing to risk my . . . my happiness again."

"*You're* not good at relationships? Em, it was your husband who was no good. You weren't to blame for what happened to your marriage."

"I expected too much."

"You expected what you deserved and still do. A man who will love you. A man who will make you happy, who'll appreciate what you have to offer."

Emily smiled plaintively. "And what do I really have to offer, Garrett?"

Garrett cursed. "Dammit, Em, if you don't know by now, then I can't tell you. You're going to have to find it out for yourself. And when you stop being frightened of who you are, then maybe you'll realize that we should be together."

"I'm sorry," Emily said, shaking her head slowly. "But that won't happen. It—it can't."

He grabbed her shoulders and fought the urge to shake her senseless this time. But, instead, he kissed her, long and deep. "I don't believe that," he said, his breath warm against her mouth, his forehead pressed against hers. "I won't."

"Em?"

Garrett spun around to find Nora standing behind him. Her gaze darted between Garrett and Emily.

"Em, I'm ready to leave for the airport now. Our attorney is staying behind to clean up the damage. Will you be flying out with me?"

Emily nodded and stepped out of Garrett's embrace, then walked toward Nora.

"Don't do this, Em," he warned. "Don't act like last night didn't mean anything. You can't just forget what happened between us."

She stopped short, then turned around and gave him a wavering smile. "I won't forget," she said. With that, she grabbed Nora's arm and hurried out of the conference room.

Garrett stalked to the door and watched them as they both rushed down the hall. He swore silently, then raked his fingers through his hair and pressed the heels of his hands into his temples.

Self-improvement? Is that what she had called what they shared together? Garrett laughed, a sound filled with resentment and anger. Such perfect irony. Maybe this was exactly what he deserved. After years of playing the capricious bachelor, breezing in and out of women's lives as if he hadn't a care in the world, never staying for too long, never bothering to commit, and never concerned with what he left behind. And now, when he'd finally found someone he wanted to spend the rest of his life with, she wanted nothing to do with him. He was the one left behind.

"Let her leave," Garrett muttered to himself. "Let her go back to her safe little world with her flower gardens and her vegetables and her fancy cooking." He didn't need her. He'd gotten along fine without Emily Taylor before he had met her, and he'd get along just fine without her now.

EMILY PUSHED THE SPADE into the soil and turned it over, exposing the rich, brown earth to the spring sun. She bent down and scooped a clump into her hand, then held it up to her nose. She loved the smell of spring, freshly turned dirt, new grass, a warm breeze off the ocean.

Since she'd returned home a week ago, she hadn't had a chance to get outside. Her garden had been left to throw off its winter coat on its own. So she'd spent most of this day digging and raking and uncovering all the green shoots that signaled another season of flowers. Her cheeks burned from the brisk wind and her loose hair was tangled with twigs and leaves. But for the first time since she'd left Garrett McCabe behind in California, she felt a glimmer of hope that her life might someday get back to normal.

The search for a new publisher had begun almost immediately upon their return. But she couldn't seem to generate any enthusiasm for the task or for the magazine. The only thing she thought about was getting back into her garden, hoping it would help her forget.

But could she ever really forget? Every waking hour refused to pass without at least one thought, one fleeting image of him. And when she closed her eyes at night, she saw him in her dreams. The distance between them didn't seem to diminish the nagging doubts that plagued her mind.

Could they have made a relationship work? Emily shook her head and dropped the clump of dirt to the ground. She tried to summon all the old anguish, the doubts and fears, and the pain she had felt at Eric's desertion. But lately, even that wasn't enough to convince her.

Garrett was different. He knew her, all her insecurities and failings. And still he accepted her for the person she was. Emily jabbed at the dirt with her spade. But hadn't her ex-husband felt the same in the beginning? Before he'd grown bored and disenchanted with their marriage? She often wondered whether he'd ever really loved her.

How was she supposed to tell if Garrett loved her? Was there some magic formula for determining whether the feelings were true and deep? Or was it just something that was felt in the furthest corners of the heart and soul? Right now, her heart felt empty, aching to be filled with something she couldn't identify.

She'd spent the past eleven years alone, without ever missing a man in her life. She'd survived, some would say thrived, and now she had everything she needed for a secure future—a home she owned, a solid career as an author, and ownership in a magazine that had grown more popular than she'd ever imagined. But none of that seemed to matter.

The future loomed ahead, filled with ordinary days and solitary nights. There was a time she had reveled in the aloneness, walking into a silent house. The silence had seemed to surround her like a cocoon, keeping her safe from the outside world.

She'd lived in that world for a long time and then she'd stepped outside into the sun and into the arms of a man she might truly love. And now, that was gone and the sun had disappeared behind a huge dark cloud. She knew from experience that if she waited long enough, the cloud would pass and she would see the sun again.

"I will be happy again," Emily chanted. "I will be happy again." She'd repeated the affirmation hundreds of times since she'd stepped on the plane in Los Angeles. If she kept saying it, maybe someday she'd believe it.

"I will be happy again," she shouted to the treetops, punctuating the sentence with her spade. "I will be happy again."

"I certainly hope so!" a cry came back.

Emily looked up from her garden to find Nora standing next to the house, dressed in a bulky coat, dirty jeans and a pair of muddy duck shoes. Emily waved and Nora trudged across the lawn toward her.

"What are you doing here?"

"I brought a little gift to cheer you up," Nora called.

"A gift?" Emily smiled.

"Sheep manure," Nora said. She stopped beside Emily and surveyed the state of her garden. "It's good stuff, right from the sheep to your front door. It's in the back of my pickup. Where do you want me to put it?"

"Not at my front door!" Emily cried. "You can drive the truck right back here and we'll dump it along the fence."

Nora grabbed the spade from Emily's hand. "So, how's it going?"

Emily nodded. "Good. I took care of the roses and all my perennials are coming up. A few more—"

"That's not what I meant, Em."

Emily bit her bottom lip, wavering under Nora's discerning gaze. "I'm doing fine."

"Have you heard from him?"

Emily shook her head. "I don't expect I will. He's got his life, I've got mine."

"He doesn't have a job anymore," Nora said. "Thanks to you."

"Me?" Emily gasped. "I'm not to blame for that!"

Nora raised a questioning brow. "You aren't? He gave up his job to keep you from signing that deal."

"How do we even know what he said was true? We don't know that Parker was trying to cheat us."

"I think he was, Em. Our attorney went over the contract that Garrett ripped up. Then he contacted some of Parker's former business associates, people he'd duped and cheated out of their share of their magazines. He's a very clever man, and he wouldn't have stopped until he got exactly what he wanted—complete control of *At Home*. Garrett was right. Parker was up to no good and he never had any intention of keeping us on staff any longer than necessary."

"But Garrett lied to me," Emily said.

"How did he lie to you? He withheld the truth a little longer than you liked. He was just trying to protect you."

"He could have told me about Parker earlier," Emily said.

"Aren't you just using that as an excuse, Em?" Nora said.

"Why are you defending him?" Emily asked, her voice laced with irritation. "I thought you had decided he was just like Eric."

"Any man who'd ride to your defense like he did does not deserve the designation of slimeball in my book."

Emily sighed and grabbed her spade from Nora's hand, then returned to digging in the garden.

"What's the real reason you're pushing him out of your life, Em?"

She stopped digging and stared down at the dirt she'd turned over. "I'm afraid."

"Of what?"

She braced her arm on the spade and turned back to Nora. "I'm afraid that Garrett will discover the same thing that Eric did. That he will start out loving me, but then he'll have to leave. Eric said he loved me, Nora, and I truly believed he did when he married me. But something happened in the five years that we were together. Who's to say that the same thing wouldn't happen with Garrett, that he wouldn't feel compelled to leave, too?"

"No one can offer you guarantees, Em. You just have to trust your heart. And trust Garrett."

"Garrett doesn't love me," she said softly. "He's not the kind to settle down and get married. He took our night together exactly as I did—one night. It's over, Nora. For both Garrett and me. And it's time I got on with my life."

"If that's what you believe, then all the sheep manure in the world isn't going to make you feel any better," Nora said with a grin.

Emily giggled and wiped an errant tear from her cheek. "Maybe not. But a few bags of peat moss would help."

Nora put her arm around Emily's shoulders. "Come on. Let's unload the truck and we'll go into town and treat you to a few bags."

Emily stopped, then threw her arms around Nora's neck. "You're the best friend I could ever ask for, Nora."

She patted Emily on the back. "I know, I know. It's a tough job, but someone's got to do it."

Emily drew back and smiled at her friend. She already did feel a little better. And a trip to the garden center was guaranteed to lift her spirits even further. Shopping for seeds would be just the thing to keep her mind off Garrett McCabe.

"ADD FLAVOR PACKAGE to drained macaroni," Garrett murmured.

He looked down into the pan then back up at the box. This was supposed to be easy. Josh Banks used to make macaroni and cheese from a box all the time. But this didn't look quite right. First, the macaroni looked a lot bigger than he had remembered. And how was he supposed to drain it when there wasn't any water left in the pan? Maybe it was all hiding inside those little tubes. Shrugging, he ripped open the package and stirred in the orange-colored powder, then dumped in a healthy measure of milk and a blob of butter.

"It looks like macaroni soup," he said. He picked up the box again, then placed the pan back on the stove. "Maybe it needs to cook a little more."

Garrett peeked through the door of the microwave at the hot dogs he had put inside ten minutes before. But to his dismay, they no longer looked like hot dogs. In fact, very little resembling a hot dog remained on the plate. He popped open the door. Somehow, they'd exploded and little pieces of his main course now clung tenaciously to the inside of the oven. He'd worked the microwave at the *Post* many times, but this one was much more complex. In the effort to get it to turn on, he'd probably pushed the Explode setting by mistake.

"Maybe this wasn't such a great idea," he admitted out loud.

He glanced around at the disaster that had befallen Emily's tidy kitchen. In the hour since Nora had let him in the front door, he'd managed to destroy the pristine order of nearly every countertop and cupboard in the place. The stovetop and microwave were a mess. And the floor didn't look so great, either. This little dinner would definitely be a surprise to Emily, but he wasn't sure it would be for the right reason.

Still, he was determined to make this dinner work. Emily had planned a romantic meal for them and look where it had led. And now, he would do the same. And if he was lucky, a main course of hot dogs and macaroni and cheese would help pave the way to a new start for them both.

He glanced at his watch. Emily was due home from the office at seven. He had just ten minutes to clean up before she arrived. Garrett wiped his hands on the gingham chef's apron he wore, then stepped over to the sink and flipped on the light switch. But instead of illumination, he got only a loud grinding sound from sink. He flipped the switch off and on again, then stared down into the sink. The handle of a wooden spoon bounced around in the drain. He pulled it out to find the business end completely shredded.

"Garbage disposal," he murmured. "Smart, McCabe." He shut the thing off then shoved the spoon into the nearest drawer. Grabbing the bottle of wine he'd uncorked, he decided to take his first complete tour of her house.

She owned a lovely piece of property halfway between Middletown and Newport. Her roomy Cape Cod cottage was a reflection of the woman she was, bright and beautiful, warm and cheery. Every piece of furniture in the living room, every picture and knickknack looked as if it had been chosen with great care. Oddly enough, Garrett felt more at home here than he'd ever felt in his own apartment. Maybe it was because he was surrounded by all the things that Emily loved. He could feel her presence even when she wasn't around.

He wandered into the bedroom, stopping to stare at the huge, carved four-poster bed. Then he walked over to it and pulled the covers back. A chuckle rumbled in his chest. Flowered sheets. Somehow, it didn't make a difference anymore. He didn't care what he slept on as long as he had Emily beside him every night.

He looked at the office next and then the spare bedroom, before the tour ended in Emily's dining room. There, he realized he hadn't even gotten to the table yet. Garrett pulled out a chair and sat down, then took a long drink right out of the wine bottle.

Rubbing his eyes, he slouched down in the chair. Twenty-four hours without sleep. He'd left L.A. two weeks behind Emily, two weeks after the meeting in Parker's office. It had been two weeks of hell being away from her, but he knew the time apart would give her the time she needed to realize her true feelings for him. He only hoped that she'd missed him as much as he'd missed her.

The flight took him directly into Boston for an interview with the editor of the *Globe*. Four hours later, he had a job offer and everything he needed to make Emily part of his life again.

On a whim, he had called Nora at the *At Home* offices on his way out of Boston, asking for directions to Emily's house and hoping for news about her state of mind. He wasn't sure just how happy Emily might be to see him and he wasn't about to risk it. The dinner had been an afterthought, but Nora was willing to help and offered him a way into Emily's house. Garrett glanced into the kitchen. Upon further consideration, dinner probably should have remained an afterthought.

Garrett sighed and closed his eyes. He should have trusted himself with no more than takeout. But he had wanted to make this meal to prove a point. In a way, he wanted to prove to her that he understood and respected what she did. And if Emily wanted a man who'd participate in every aspect of a relationship, he was going to show her that he was just that man. Though he wasn't sure she'd ever let him near her kitchen again. Or her garden or her—

An ear-splitting shriek echoed through the house. In one swift movement, Garrett shot to his feet, the chair crashing backward behind him. He hurried into the kitchen, wondering if he'd somehow managed to set off the smoke alarm. But the only fire he found was the fire in Emily's eyes as she stood inside the back door.

He grinned and waved. "Hi, honey. How was your day?"

She gave another tiny shriek when she saw him standing on the far side of the kitchen. "What—what are you doing here?" she demanded. "How did you get in?" She moaned and stepped over to the counter, running her finger through the instant pudding mix he'd spilled earlier. "And who did this to my kitchen?" She lifted her foot up from the floor and looked at the bottom of her shoe. She'd obviously found the spot where he'd spilled the can of chocolate syrup.

She looked more beautiful than he'd remembered. Her coppery hair was tumbled down around her face in a mass of curls, blown wild by the wind. He instantly recalled how it felt between his fingers and he fought the temptation to walk right over to her and pull her into his arms.

"I'm sorry about the kitchen," Garrett said. "I was hoping to get it cleaned up before you got home."

"You're sorry? You broke into my house, destroyed my kitchen and all you can say is you're sorry?"

"I didn't break into your house, Em. Nora let me in."

"Nora?" Emily swore out loud, surprising Garrett with her knowledge of the vernacular. "When is she going to learn to stay out of my life?"

"Maybe she knows what's best for you," Garrett said.

"Well, she doesn't have to spend the next week cleaning up the mess you made, does she?"

He grinned at her. "She knows how much you missed me," Garrett said teasingly.

"I didn't miss you. So don't try to turn on the charm with me, Garrett McCabe. It won't work."

He slowly approached and she backed away, putting the huge butcher block in the center of the kitchen between them. "You did miss me, didn't you?" he asked.

"No," she said. She grabbed an apple from a basket on the counter and drew her arm back.

"Emily, Emily. Are you going to resort to throwing fruits and vegetables again?"

"I want you to get out of my house," she ordered. "Now."

He moved to the right and she responded, still using the butcher block as protection. "Em, what happened in Parker's office didn't change the way I feel about you and I don't think it changed the way you feel about me."

"How do you know how I feel?" she said.

"You're in love with me," Garrett said, as if it were fact.

Emily laughed. "I am not," she said.

"And I love you."

She froze, her eyes wide with astonishment. She lowered her arm and the apple dropped to the floor, bounced two times, then disappeared beneath the butcher block.

"It's true," he said. "I do love you."

"How—how do you know?" she asked softly.

"Because I've never really loved any woman in my entire life. Until you. It's like I have no doubts, Em. It's all there, right in front of me, and I can't deny it. And I don't think you can, either."

"Say it again," Emily said, her gaze fixed on his face as if she were trying to discern the truth in his words.

"I love you." Garrett tipped his head back and laughed. "I love Emily Taylor!" he shouted. "And I want everyone to know it."

She waited for a long moment, watching him. And then she spoke. "And she loves you," she replied.

Garrett opened his arms wide and she stepped around the butcher block, right into his embrace. He kissed her, soft and sweet, and filled with all the longing of the past few weeks. She giggled as he rained tiny kisses over her eyes and cheeks before finally settling on her mouth again.

Then she pulled back and sniffed the air. "What *is* that smell?" She pulled out of his embrace and walked over to the stove, then looked inside the pan. "Oh, dear." She switched off the burner then picked the pan up and turned it upside down. Nothing came out. "What was this?"

Garrett came up behind her and wrapped his arms around her waist. "Dinner."

She shook her head. "Please, please promise me you won't ever step into my kitchen again without fair warning."

"Well, that's going to be a little hard to promise."

She turned around in his arms. "Why?"

"Because we have to get married," Garrett explained. "And when we get married, I plan to do half the cooking."

"What?" Emily gasped.

"I think it's only fair that we share the household duties, don't you think?"

"No, no. Repeat what you just said. Before the cooking part."

"We have to get married?" Garrett repeated.

"Is this your idea of a proposal?" she asked in disbelief.

Garrett sighed. "I suppose you want me to do it the proper way."

Emily nodded.

He struggled down to one knee and looked up at her, then grabbed her right hand and clasped it in his. "Emily Taylor, will you marry me?"

She watched him with sparkling green eyes, her lips curled in a mischievous smile. "Why should I marry you, Garrett McCabe?"

He cleared his throat and put on a serious face. "Because I love you and I want to spend the rest of my life with you." He paused and frowned. "Oh, and because I agreed to write a column on married life for the *Boston Globe*."

Emily shook her head and laughed. "You are terrible. What am I going to do with you?"

Garrett tugged her down onto the floor and pulled her into his arms. "Well, we're in a kitchen," he teased, nibbling on her earlobe. She moaned softly. "And we're both adults." He kissed the hollow of her throat and he heard her breath catch. "And we do make our own rules."

"Hmm," she replied.

He watched her face until she opened her eyes. "Why don't you try seducing me again?"

Epilogue

FLYNN'S WAS NEARLY EMPTY when they walked in. Garrett waved at Eddie and Bob and then took Emily's hand and led her to the poker table in the back room. Tru followed him, his arm around Caroline's shoulders, and Josh pulled Taryn by the hand. They all sat down at their favorite table and Eddie appeared to take their drink orders. Bob trailed behind him.

"So what's new, boys and girls?" Eddie said. "I haven't seen any of you in here for a long time."

Taryn jumped up and placed her hand on Josh's shoulder. "Josh and I have some news," she offered. "We gave up the apartment at the Arms and we're leaving for Europe next week. I'm going to study painting for a few months with my old teacher and Josh is going to learn French and visit with his good friend, Berti. And we're going to live in an attic on the Left Bank."

Emily sighed. "That sounds so romantic."

Garrett leaned over. "When we get home, we'll move our bed up to the attic, if you'd like."

Emily giggled and slapped Garrett on the arm. "It wouldn't be the same as Paris."

Tru leaned back in his chair. "We've got some news. Caroline, tell Eddie what's new."

Caroline smiled and grabbed her husband's hand. "Tru and I are going to have a baby. That's what's new."

"A baby!" Taryn shrieked. "Did you hear that Josh? Tru and Caroline are going to have a baby. Why didn't you tell me?" She jumped to her feet and scurried around the table, then threw her arms around Caroline's neck. On her way back to her chair, she threw her arms around Tru and gave him a hug, too. "You'll make a wonderful daddy, Truman."

Emily reached across the table and squeezed Caroline's hand. "Congratulations, Caroline. This is wonderful news."

Tru turned to Garrett. "So what's your news, McCabe?"

"Well, Em, what is our news? We must have some news or we wouldn't have flown all the way back here. Now, what was it?"

"Don't tease," Emily said, linking her arm in Garrett's. "Our news is that Garrett and I are getting married."

Taryn jumped up again and hugged Emily this time. "That's wonderful! Did you hear that, Josh? Emily and Garrett are getting married. When?"

"Today," Garrett said. "At Descanso Gardens at two o'clock. And you're all invited. Bob and Eddie, too. And Eddie, you should be sure to bring Kim. Everyone from the building is invited."

"Eddie, bring us drinks all around," Tru said. "Champagne for all of us, and for my lovely wife, a glass of milk. I have a toast to make."

Eddie hurried off to the bar and returned a few moments later with the drinks. When they were all distributed, Tru held his glass up. "To the lady in the mirror!"

Josh and Garrett raised their glasses at the center of the table and clicked them together. Then, they all downed their champagne in one long drink.

"The lady in the mirror?" Emily said, turning to her fiancé. "What lady?"

Garrett smiled at her. "It's just a silly old legend about a mirror. And something to do with dreams and fears."

Caroline frowned. "I've never heard the story. What is it?"

"There's supposed to be a mirror in apartment 1-G at the Bachelor Arms," Taryn explained. "It's supposed to have some mysterious powers. I've never really gotten the whole story. Have you seen the mirror, Josh?"

Josh blinked at his wife from behind his wire-rimmed glasses. "I've never seen the mirror," he said. "What about you, Tru?"

Tru smiled and shrugged. "Not me. Garrett? Have you seen the mirror?"

"Nope. It's just an old story that says if you see this woman's image in this old mirror, your deepest fear or your greatest dream will come true. I don't even think there is a mirror."

Emily shivered. "That's kind of spooky, isn't it?"

"You know what's really spooky?" Caroline said. "Not too long ago, all you guys were bachelors. And look at you now. Bachelors no more."

Emily picked up her glass and held it out in the center of the table. Taryn followed suit and then Caroline. "To our bachelors and the Bachelor Arms," she said softly. "And to the lady in the mirror, whoever she is."

COMING UP IN
BACHELOR ARMS

When Blythe Fielding planned her wedding and asked her two best friends, Caitlin and Lily, to be bridesmaids, none of them had a clue a new romance was around the corner for each of them—even the bride! These entertaining, dramatic stories of friendship, mystery and love by JoAnn Ross continue the exploits of the residents of Bachelor Arms and answer one very important question: Will Blythe ever walk down the aisle? Find out in:

Never a Bride (May 1995, #537)
For Richer or Poorer (June 1995, #541)
Three Grooms and a Wedding (July 1995, #545)

Soon to move into Bachelor Arms are the heroes and heroines in books by always-popular Candace Schuler and Judith Arnold. Don't miss their stories!

HARLEQUIN®

Temptation®

Secret Fantasies

Do you have a secret fantasy?

Small-town waitress Ellen Montrose does. At night she dreams of the Whitfield mansion, of dancing in the ballroom with a handsome sexy stranger. But fantasy and reality start to mysteriously collide when Ellen meets the man of her dreams—in the flesh—at the diner. Enjoy #538 THE MAN FROM SHADOW VALLEY by Regan Forest, available in May 1995.

Everybody has a secret fantasy. And you'll find them all in Temptation's exciting new yearlong miniseries— Secret Fantasies. Beginning January 1995, one book each month focuses on the hero or heroine's innermost romantic desires....

SF-5

MILLION DOLLAR SWEEPSTAKES (III)

No purchase necessary. To enter the sweepstakes and receive the Free Books and Surprise Gift, follow the directions published and complete and mail your "Win A Fortune" Game Card. If not taking advantage of the book and gift offer or if the "Win A Fortune" Game Card is missing, you may enter by hand-printing your name and address on a 3" X 5" card and mailing it (limit: one entry per envelope) via First Class Mail to: Million Dollar Sweepstakes (III) "Win A Fortune" Game, P.O. Box 1867, Buffalo, NY 14269-1867, or Million Dollar Sweepstakes (III) "Win A Fortune" Game, P.O. Box 609, Fort Erie, Ontario L2A 5X3. When your entry is received, you will be assigned sweepstakes numbers. To be eligible entries must be received no later than March 31, 1996. No liability is assumed for printing errors or lost, late or misdirected entries. Odds of winning are determined by the number of eligible entries distributed and received.

Sweepstakes open to residents of the U.S. (except Puerto Rico), Canada, Europe and Taiwan who are 18 years of age or older. All applicable laws and regulations apply. Sweepstakes offer void wherever prohibited by law. Values of all prizes are in U.S. currency. This sweepstakes is presented by Torstar Corp, its subsidiaries and affiliates, in conjunction with book, merchandise and/or product offerings. For a copy of the official rules governing this sweepstakes offer, send a self-addressed, stamped envelope (WA residents need not affix return postage) to: MILLION DOLLAR SWEEPSTAKES (III) Rules, P.O. Box 4573, Blair, NE 68009, USA.

SWP-H495

MOVE OVER, MELROSE PLACE!

Apartment for rent
One bedroom
Bachelor Arms
555-1234

Come live and love in L.A. with the tenants of Bachelor Arms. Enjoy a year's worth of wonderful love stories and meet colorful neighbors you'll bump into again and again.

When Blythe Fielding planned her wedding and asked her two best friends, Caitlin and Lily, to be bridesmaids, none of them knew a new romance was around the corner for each of them—not even the bride! These entertaining, dramatic stories of friendship, mystery and love by JoAnn Ross continue the exploits of the residents of Bachelor Arms and answer one very important question: Will Blythe ever get to walk down the aisle? Find out in:

NEVER A BRIDE (May 1995) #537

FOR RICHER OR POORER (June 1995) #541

THREE GROOMS AND A WEDDING (July 1995) #545

Soon to move into Bachelor Arms are the heroes and heroines in books by always popular Candace Schuler and Judith Arnold. A new book every month!

Don't miss the goings-on at Bachelor Arms.

BA4

THREE GROOMS:
Case, Carter and Mike

TWO WORDS:
"We Don't!"

ONE MINISERIES:

GROOMS ON THE RUN

Starting in May 1995, Harlequin Temptation
brings you an exciting miniseries called

GROOMS ON THE RUN

Each book (and there'll be one a month for three
months!) features a sexy hero who's ready to say,
"I do!" but ends up saying, "I don't!"

Watch for these special Temptations:

In May, **I WON'T!** by Gina Wilkins #539
In June, **JILT TRIP** by Heather MacAllister #543
In July, **NOT THIS GUY!** by Glenda Sanders #547

Available wherever Harlequin books are sold.

GROOMS-1

Harlequin invites you to the most romantic
wedding of the season...with

MARRY ME, COWBOY!

And you could WIN A DREAM VACATION of a lifetime!

from HARLEQUIN BOOKS and SANDALS—
THE CARIBBEAN'S #1 **ULTRA INCLUSIVE**℠ LUXURY RESORTS
FOR COUPLES ONLY.

Harlequin Books and Sandals Resorts are offering you a
vacation of a lifetime—a vacation of your choice at any of
the Sandals Caribbean resorts—FREE!

LOOK FOR FURTHER DETAILS in the Harlequin Books
title MARRY ME, COWBOY!, an exciting collection
of four brand-new short stories by popular romance
authors, including *New York Times* bestselling author
JANET DAILEY!

**AVAILABLE IN APRIL WHEREVER
HARLEQUIN BOOKS ARE SOLD.**

HARLEQUIN® & *Sandals*®

MMC-SANDT

HARLEQUIN®

Temptation

BACHELOR ARMS SURVEY

Vote for Your Favorite!

If all these guys were bachelors, who would you most want to catch? Please! Just choose one from this delectable dozen!

1 ☐ Mel Gibson
2 ☐ Sean Connery
3 ☐ Kevin Costner
4 ☐ Alec Baldwin
5 ☐ Denzel Washington
6 ☐ Tom Cruise
7 ☐ Andre Agassi
8 ☐ Michael Jordan
9 ☐ Jack Nicholson
10 ☐ Robert Redford
11 ☐ Paul Newman
12 ☐ Keanu Reeves

We want to hear from you, so please send in your response to:

In the U.S.: BACHELOR ARMS,
P.O. Box 9076, Buffalo, NY 14269-9076
In Canada: BACHELOR ARMS,
P.O. Box 637, Ft. Erie, ON L2A 5X3

Name: _____

Address _____ City: _____

State/Prov.: _____ Zip/Postal Code: _____

Please note that all entries become the property of Harlequin and we may publish them in any publication, with credit at our discretion.

HTBA